TOPLINER REDSTARS

The Doubting Kind

Part Two: All Who Love Us...

Alison Prince

Macmillan

First published by Methuen Children's Books Ltd 1975

Published in *Topliner Redstars* in 1977 by
MACMILLAN EDUCATION LTD
Houndmills Basingstoke Hampshire RG21 2XS
and London
Associated companies in New York Dublin
Melbourne Johannesburg and Delhi

Printed in Great Britain by
RICHARD CLAY (THE CHAUCER PRESS) LTD
Bungay Suffolk

Contents

4 Thursday

Bobbie woke from a confused dream about a many-roomed prison in which she ran like a rat in a maze from cell to cell, confronted by door after door. The image of prison persisted in her first waking moments, for she opened her eyes in almost total darkness and then perceived dim squares of faint grey light, high up, like the windows of a cell.

Windows. A big room. Not a prison, then, Bobbie realised with relief. She was in the warehouse where the Brethren lived. Memory returned, reassuringly at first and then with dismay. What a mess she had made of things! And what a lot of dreadful explaining she would have to do.

Suddenly Bobbie wished she was back in her own warm, pretty bedroom, snug between the pink sheets instead of lying here, cramped and stiff, with the dusty stickiness that comes of sleeping in one's clothes. She sat up. Nearly all the beds were occupied, but in the dim light Bobbie was not sure of the age or sex of the sleepers. Some, to judge by the smallness of the humps under the bedclothes, were children. Small mounds of earth, they looked like, in a churchyard. With small coffins underneath. Small, rotting bodies.... Oh, no. Bobbie shook her head hard. Early morning was a bad time for the horrors. They took you at a disadvantage while you were weak and only half alive.

What would happen today? Gideon would have been to see Bobbie's mother if he had kept his promise of last night. What could their meeting have been like? She decided not to think about it. And what would her father say if he came out of hospital to find Bobbie away from home? Oh, it was going to be terrible. Her mother would arrive quite soon, and she would have told Miss Beacon where Bobbie was, and probably the police, too. Or perhaps the police had already talked to Miss Beacon. 'What kind of girl *is* this, madam? Untrustworthy you say? And disobedient? Stole this jersey, did she? And smashed a window?' It would all be written down, painstakingly. 'Ran – away – from – school.' And then it would be read out before some awful woman in a hat. They didn't have judges, did they, for young offenders?

Young offenders, young offenders. The phrase echoed ominously. Have I offended Thee, oh Lord? Oh, Lord, Lord, are you there to be offended? Suddenly Bobbie was acutely aware of the frightening solitude of doubt. In the desolate half-light of dawn, the gentle, bearded, Sunday-school face of Jesus was no more than a pretty picture by some unknown man who, like Bobbie, had wanted the Lord to exist. In truth it seemed more likely that there was nothing. No plan, no guidance, no standards – just a random chemical accident, as Fanny contended. The Spirit of God had not moved upon the waters and created life; it was man himself, out of the fear of his own insignificance, who had created God.

Bobbie, sitting hunched up on the small iron bed, put her head down on her knees in dry-eyed misery. Soon the Brethren would begin to get up and go about their slow, calm business. 'God loves you,' they would greet her – and how could she respond? Without a true belief, it would be cheating to stay here. She had better go home and face whatever dreadfulness had to be faced. There was nothing left except endurance, and so there was no point in delay.

She lay back on the bed, hands behind her head, and gazed up at the high ceiling, remembering an argument she had once had with Fanny. 'I don't know why you worry, Bob,' Fanny had said. 'Whyever does it matter if there's a God or not? If you ask me, everybody is their own God – and anyway, there's such a lot to *do*.' And Bobbie had answered, 'I'd feel so alone if I thought there was nothing there at all.' And now, in this dormitory full of sleeping strangers, the loneliness which she had dreaded was very real.

Bobbie looked at her watch but the grey light was too faint for her to see the hands. Perhaps she had better try to go back to sleep for a while. She lay back and turned on her side. After what seemed quite a long time she felt more wide awake than ever. The blanket was scratchy and Bobbie was pressingly aware of the fact that she had a full bladder. It was a long time since Ruth had led her up the stone stairs to bed last night and shown her the little toilet adjacent to the dormitory.

At last Bobbie could bear it no longer. She sat up, fished for her shoes under the bed and pushed her feet into them. Then she put her skirt on and tiptoed cautiously across the floor.

She felt very much better when she had used the lavatory and washed her hands and face in the tiny corner basin with its one cold tap. She went back to the dormitory and pushed open the door. The air which met her smelt frowsily of sleeping people, warm and sticky and unexpectedly repulsive. Bobbie withdrew her head and let the door swing shut again. She could not go back in there. What should she do? She stood irresolute for a moment. Perhaps there was some coffee downstairs. They wouldn't mind if she helped herself, would they? Oh, and she must give them some money for the food last night and the bed. It was only fair.

Bobbie went quietly down the stone steps – then stiffened. She could hear voices downstairs. Before she could move, a door opened and a bright shaft of light pinned her like a fly in amber. 'Hello!' said Gideon, unsurprised. 'God loves you — aren't you up early! Do you want some coffee?'

'Yes, please,' said Bobbie. That was the nice thing about the Brethren. They didn't ask questions or seem disapproving about anything.

In the big room, several young men were drinking coffee and eating hunks of bread and jam. 'We're just off to market,' announced Jeremiah with his mouth full.

'But the shops won't be open yet, will they?' asked Bobbie.

He laughed. 'That's the point. We're going up to the market. They've just about finished trading by now and we get the left-overs. Trimmings, bruised fruit – a bit of this and that. We use it the same day, so it's fine.'

'Oh, I see.' Bobbie was abashed by Jeremiah's clear-eyed stare. 'I'm awfully sorry I didn't come down again last night,' she said. 'I meant to come and listen to you playing your trumpet but I never woke up until this morning.'

'I didn't play last night,' said Jeremiah. 'We thought it might wake you.'

'Oh.' Bobbie was even more confused. 'That was very kind of you – but you shouldn't have not played just because of me.'

'All time is the Lord's,' said Jeremiah calmly. 'There are plenty more evenings.'

'Coffee,' said Gideon, offering a steaming mug.

'Oh, thank you.' Bobbie stirred and sipped. Then she thought of something. 'Gideon – did you go round to see my mother last night? Ruth said. . . .'

'Yes, I went,' said Gideon. 'I found the house all right, and I knocked and rang lots of times, but I couldn't make anyone hear. The house was all in darkness. I don't know if your mother was asleep or what. It wasn't very late.'

Bobbie's heart sank. 'Mum doesn't always answer the door,' she said awkwardly. 'Not if she's drunk she doesn't.'

'Well, I had a pencil, so I wrote on the back of the bit of paper I had, "Your daughter is safe with us, praise the Lord", and put our address on it. Then I pushed it into the letter box. I left it sort of gripped half-way so it wouldn't go under the mat or anything and it would be more noticeable. I mean, I knew it was important.'

'Thank you,' said Bobbie.

'It is the Lord you must thank,' said Gideon. 'I only do His will.'

Bobbie sighed. 'I wish I was sure,' she said. The young men nodded understandingly. 'It isn't easy,' said Jeremiah. 'That's what the Lord asks of us in return for His goodness – that we make the big effort to trust Him.'

'Knowing you are unsure is the first step,' said a boy called Amos. 'It's the beginning of understanding what He asks.'

'Is it?' Bobbie looked wretched. 'I'm not even certain of that.'

'It's terribly hard at first,' said Gideon. 'If you thought it was easy then it wouldn't be worth anything, would it? Now look, what are you going to do? This morning, I mean – right now?'

'I don't know. I thought I ought to go home, really.'

'Your mother won't be up yet. It's hardly light.'

'Why don't you come to the market with us?' suggested Jeremiah. 'It's not six o'clock yet – we'll be there and back in a couple of hours and then you can think what to do when everyone's awake. The Lord will guide you. Come on – there's heaps of room in the ambulance.'

Problems seemed to solve themselves wonderfully simply when the Brethren were about, Bobbie thought. Aloud, she said, 'If you're sure I won't be in the way. . . .'

'Not a bit – it's good having a girl because we get more stuff,' said Amos. 'Do you know everyone, by the way? Jeremiah you know – Gideon – and these are Paul and Ezekiel.'

'You must have a name in God,' said Gideon to Bobbie. 'Ruth will think of one. But we'll call you Bobbie for now. Come on – let's go.'

Sylvia woke up confused in the early dawn, to find herself in a strange room. Marjorie was bending over her, shaking her by the arm.

'Mum! Listen, dear – I think you'd better come. Sister says. . . .'

'Oh, God.' Hospital. Phone call. Gordon driving them to the hospital last night. that's right. David. 'Is this – it?'

'I'm afraid it looks as if he's going, dear. Sister says you should come now if you want to be with him.'

'I can't,' said Sylvia abruptly. She sat up on the hospital bed, clutching a red blanket round her, waif-like, her fingers tight on its bright fluffiness. Her face crumpled with a kind of nausea. 'Marjorie, I *can't* go in there.'

'No, of course not,' said Marjorie in her professionally re-assuring voice. 'Sister will understand. You stay here.' But she did not look at her mother as she left the room.

For a moment Sylvia stared at the silently closing door then she jumped up, snatched it open and stared out along the brightly-lit corridor in time to see her daughter slip quietly through the double doors into the ward. Then the corridor was empty. There was no sound.

Sylvia stood motionless in the doorway and dug her nails into the palms of her hands. He mustn't go. Not like this, without saying anything. Not with so many misunderstandings. Tears began to pour down Sylvia's face. David. David. She ran blindly down the corridor and thrust her way through the doors into the ward, which was dimly lit except for the glare of light behind the pink flowered curtains round David's bed.

'Sister! Please, I must tell him. . . .'

'Ssh!'

The Night Sister came out from behind the screens and Sylvia glimpsed white coated figures, frightening rubber tubes, gas cylinders. They seemed to be tidying up. Putting things away. A doctor was taking off his mask. David's face was covered.

The nurse put her hand on Sylvia's arm. 'I'm sorry, my dear.'

Sorry?

'No,' protested Sylvia. 'No.'

'Your daughter did tell you it was critical, didn't she? I know she went to fetch you.'

'Yes, she did.' A bitter mirth invaded Sylvia's agony. 'I bloody well – missed the boat. Didn't I?' And then the tears destroyed all words and although she was ashamed of the raucous, ugly noises she was making she could not stop them and made no protest when the Night Sister took her by the arm and led her gently out of the ward.

When Marjorie rang up from the hospital, Gordon assumed the worst. It was no good kidding oneself. A man with a ruptured spleen sounded like trouble. Pity they hadn't diagnosed it earlier, but if he was deeply unconscious. . . .

'– At about half past six this morning,' Marjorie was saying.

'About an hour ago. M'm, I was afraid it looked bad. I'm

awfully sorry though, love. Are you all right?'

'Yes, I'm all right.' Marjorie's voice sounded momentarily wobbly but she recovered control quickly. 'It's Mother I'm worried about. She's collapsed completely – just keeps crying and crying. They've given her a mild sedative but....'

'Look, I'll come and fetch you. Sorry, it must seem as if I deserted the sinking ship last night but there really wasn't much I could do at the hospital. And I don't like Keron not having one of us here when he wakes in the morning, Mrs Elkin or no Mrs Elkin.'

'How is he?'

'Oh, fine. Shovelling up Weetabix. Mrs E is here, of course – mortally offended that I came back last night. She's just on her third cup of tea.'

'Is she going to take him to nursery school?'

'I haven't asked her. It's a hell of a long way on foot. What time do they open?'

'Eight o'clock. I usually drop him at twenty to nine but it doesn't matter if he's early.'

'OK. Leave it to me. I'll take him round there and then come on to you. Don't worry if I'm a bit late – it'll be rush hour.'

'Gordon, is there any news about Bobbie?'

''Fraid not. I rang the police last night but they hadn't heard anything. I gave them this number in case anything cropped up during the night but they haven't rung. It's very early, though. You mustn't worry. I bet she's gone to stay with a friend and she'll turn up at school as if nothing had happened.'

'I hope so,' said Marjorie, sounding doubtful. 'Can you call in at the house, though, just in case she's there? I rang just before I rang you and there was no reply but she *might* be in bed asleep. She doesn't know about Dad, you see. She may not even realise that Mum's not there.'

'All right,' Gordon promised. 'I'll drop in. Now, you look after yourself – have you been up all night?'

'More or less.'

'God, you must feel terrible. Try and get a bit of kip. I'll be there as soon as I can. Oh, and I'll ring the surgery and tell them they'll have to manage without you.'

When Marjorie had rung off, Gordon sighed. He made a mental note to buy a bottle of gin as soon as the shops opened. Whatever today brought forth, it looked as if somebody was going to need it – even if it was only Gordon himself.

'You with this load of Jesus freaks, are you?' asked the man with the oranges.

'Sort of,' said Bobbie. It was wonderful here in the market, daylight now but still yellow-lit from the huge electric bulbs in their flat white shades like enamel plates.

' 'Ere. 'Ow d'you go on, then?' The man with the oranges leaned confidentially across a pile of Jaffa crates to breathe his early-morning-licensed beer fumes over Bobbie.

'What do you mean?'

'Well, money and that. Nobody can't live on bloody cabbage stalks now, can they? 'Oo provides the ackers?'

'I don't really know. Everyone sort of shares whatever there is.'

'Yes, but 'ows it *get* there? Them young fellers you're with, they ain't no walkin' skelingtons, are they? Not exactly starvin'. Now, it costs money, feedin' young chaps like that. *'Oo's* money?'

'I know it sounds silly,' said Bobbie, 'but I honestly don't know. I don't really belong, you see. I'm just sort of – visiting. But they've been awfully kind. Look, I've fifty pence and I feel I owe them something. Do you think I could buy some fruit from you for that? Or isn't it enough?'

The man with the oranges rubbed his chin consideringly. 'Tell you what I'll do for yer. I'll do yer a half box of Moroccans. Now, they're not bad at all, yer Moroccans. 'Ere.'

With a box opener he levered the slats off the top of a crate and took an orange out of its pink tissue wrappings. 'Good little orange at the price, is that.'

'They look lovely. Thank you very much.' Bobbie gave the man fifty pence, in four tens and two fives. He looked at it, then banged the slats roughly back into place on the top of the crate. ' 'Ere,' he said, ' 'ave the 'ole crate. I want me 'ead read, but still.'

Bobbie glowed. 'Oh, you *are* lovely! Thank you *ever* so much!' She turned and waved at the boys who were lugging a large sack full of cabbage trimmings. 'Amos! Gideon! Come and look here!' They came across. 'Look what I've got!' said Bobbie triumphantly. 'A whole crate of oranges from this kind man!'

'Thank you, Lord,' said Amos respectfully.

'Amen,' said Gideon.

'Think nothink of it,' said the man with the oranges.

Between them the boys picked up the crate and carried it away to the old ambulance, leaving the less precious sack for a second journey. 'And thank you, too, brother!' Amos called over his shoulder. 'The Lord will remember you.'

'Like 'ell 'e will,' said the man cheerfully. He turned to Bobbie. 'I notice nobody thanked *you*, duck.'

'Oh, that doesn't matter,' said Bobbie. 'You're the one who's been kind. I'm sure the oranges must have cost much more than that. Look, I'd better go now.'

' 'Ang on.' The man fished about behind his crates. ' 'Ere.'

He put an immense, perfect peach into Bobbie's hand and held it there for a moment between his own hard and very dirty palms.

'That's fer you,' he said. 'Not fer sharin' among that lot. Yer a nice kid. Now get on 'ome to yer mum.' He gave her hand a final little squeeze and let it go.

Bobbie was startled and the man, seeing her colour rise, nodded with satisfaction. 'That's what I said. 'Ome to yer mum. I don't expect you like 'er – most kids don't these days. But that's where yer belong. Now, if you'll excuse me, I got work to do.' And he disappeared behind his crates.

Bobbie walked away slowly. Home to your mum. Oh, if it was only that simple. If mum was a warm, floury-handed figure in a pinny who looked up from making steak-and-kidney pudding and said, 'Hello duck – had a nice day?' Mum. How lovely to have a mum like the man meant. Don't cry. Don't be silly.

She stared down at her peach. It was almost too beautiful to eat, pinky-yellow and furry. She put it to her nose and its warm, winey smell made her mouth water. She bit into it and its juice ran overflowingly down her chin so that she had to lean forward to let it drip on the pavement instead of down her olive green cardigan. Peaches, she thought, were a wonderful anti-crying treatment.

'Hi, Bobbie!' called the boys from the ambulance where they had finished loading their haul. 'Come on! We're going now!'

Bobbie waved back with her spare hand, moving only very slowly towards them. This peach was the best one she had ever tasted and, just for these few minutes, she intended to give it her full attention. The simple pleasure of eating it dispelled her sadness and, quite suddenly, in the middle of the noisy, fragrant market with the early sunshine primrose-fresh outside, she was filled with an intoxicating sense of lightness and gaiety. This was how life should be. Now, now, it was good to be alive, here and now was the real thing and the nightmares had never been anything. Filled with a new and delirious confidence, Bobbie tossed the stone of her peach as far as she could throw it, away out of the covered market, and lost sight of it against the bright sun. The ambulance drove slowly towards her and she ran to join the boys.

Fanny's alarm clock rang at half past six. Eyes shut, she stopped it with a practised finger. Morning already. What to do today?

Bobbie.

Fanny flung back the bedclothes and got up. Of course. That's why she'd set the clock early. Must see what had happened to Bobbie. Nobody had answered the phone last night although Fanny had tried three times. It just rang and rang. Bobbie's mother might have been in bed – but it was only half past ten or maybe a bit later. You'd think she could have answered, specially when things were in such a state of drama.

Fanny dressed quickly in her school uniform. There wouldn't be time to come home again and change. She went downstairs, leaving the sleeping household to its last half hour's rest. In the kitchen she wrote on Helen's message pad, 'Gone to B's. Will go straight on to school. Love, F.' Then she washed her face under the kitchen tap, spread herself a hunk of bread and Marmite, applied a minimal quantity of make-up to her eyes, picked up her plastic bag of books and let herself out of the kitchen door, munching.

There was a piece of paper, Fanny saw, sticking out of Bobbie's letter box. She rang the bell boldly and waited. When, as she had half expected, nobody came, she pulled the piece of paper out and looked at it.

On one side, in neat capital letters, was written Bobbie's address. On the other was a message, pencilled in a large, untidy hand. 'Your daughter is safe with us. Praise the Lord. The Brethren in God, 264/266, Wilmot Road. (Near the station).' Fanny gasped. Of course. The trumpet player. Why on earth hadn't she thought of it? She ran down the path and along the road. A car approaching from behind her hooted but she ignored it and ran on. It continued to hoot and drew level with her. 'Hi!' shouted the driver, 'stop a minute!'

'What do you want?' Fanny swung round, irritated. 'I'm in a hurry!'

'I can see that! Sorry to stop you but I saw you come away from the house and I thought you might know something about Bobbie. I'm her brother-in-law. Gordon Dixon.'

'Oh! Well, look, there's this note—' Fanny leaned in through the window.

'Let me open the door,' said Gordon. 'This is no way to talk. Get in, for Heaven's sake.'

Fanny got into the car and showed Gordon the note. 'Good Lord,' he said, 'whatever does it mean? Who are these Brethren in God? Nuts of some sort?'

'Religious nuts,' assented Fanny, 'but they seem very sweet and peaceful. I'm sure they won't do Bobbie any harm. Oh, thank goodness we've found her!'

Gordon pulled away from the kerb. 'Near the station,' he muttered. 'Quickest way is down Arcot Street.' He glanced at Fanny. 'Look, are you a close friend of Bobbie's?'

17

'Oh, yes,' said Fanny confidently. 'We're absolute buddies.'

'M'm. Well, perhaps you'd be the best person to tell her.'

'Tell her what?'

Gordon frowned, clearly in some doubt as to the wisdom of his decision. 'Did you know about her father's accident?' he asked cautiously.

'Yes, I took her home after her mother had rung up the school – at least, I took her as far as the bus. Why? He isn't worse, is he?'

'He died early this morning.'

'Oh, *no*! But I thought it wasn't very serious from what Bobbie said.'

'That's what we all thought. It's obvious in retrospect that the hospital had an eye open for something more and I doubt if there's anything they could have done, but still. . . .'

'Poor Bobbie, that's awful for her. I mean, her mother's – well, she's not always in a very good mood.'

'That's one way of putting it,' said Gordon, slowing for a T-junction.

'How would you put it?' asked Fanny. Gordon glanced at her again and found his gaze returned by steady grey eyes. This girl seemed like a tough cookie, he thought to himself. For the second time in five minutes, he decided to take a risk. He didn't want to spread slander about his mother-in-law but it was important at this moment that he and this girl should understand one another.

'I think she's an alcoholic,' he said.

Fanny sighed with relief. 'That's what I think. But I don't see what we can do.'

'Oh, there's nothing we can *do*. Specially now, when she's so cut up about David. Is this the place?'

'Yes, over there. That funny brick place.'

Gordon stopped the car and switched off the ignition, then got out. Followed by Fanny, he walked across to the door and, finding no bell or knocker, banged on it with his knuckles. He and Fanny banged for a long time. At last there was a sound of fumbling at the catch and the door opened slowly to reveal a small child in a long white nightdress who stared up at them with curiosity. Fanny, staring back, could not decide whether the child was a boy or a girl. It was slim, with shoulder-length mousey-coloured hair and unexpectedly dark eyes.

'God loves you,' said the child.

'Christ!' said Gordon, clutching his head. He swallowed hard. 'Is your mummy in?' he asked the child, in a comic caricature of patience, 'or your daddy?'

'I'll get Ruth,' said the child, and pattered off.

After an even longer pause, Ruth appeared. Her long hair was unkempt and she too wore a floor-length nightdress which gave her a markedly Biblical appearance.

'God loves you,' she greeted them. Gordon ground his teeth. 'If anyone else says that to me today,' he said, 'I think I shall be sick on the spot. Where's Bobbie?'

'She was here last night,' said Ruth, unperturbed by his response, 'but she's not in her bed this morning. I looked in the bathroom and downstairs, all over – but it seems like she's gone out.'

Gordon turned grimly to Fanny. 'This is where we get the police,' he said grimly. 'Come on.'

'Just a minute,' said Fanny. She turned to Ruth. 'Have you any idea where she's gone? Did she say anything? Is she – I mean, is she all *right*?'

'She is in God's hands,' said Ruth with unshakeable calm.

'Are you *sure* she's not in there?' demanded Gordon.

'Come in and look,' invited Ruth, stepping back from the door and extending a white-sleeved arm. 'You are very welcome.'

'Oh, come on – she's obviously not there,' said Gordon to Fanny, striding back to the car. 'The thing is, Marjorie's wait-ing for me at the hospital with her mother. I *must* get going or the roads'll be jammed – I can't stop and do the detective bit.'

'That's all right,' said Fanny. 'You just go, and don't worry. I'll stay here until Bobbie comes back. There's a phone box in the station – I can ring her house, too, in case she's gone there. Most probably that's just what she's done, and we've missed her on the way. She'd go over the footbridge, you see.'

Gordon got into his car but did not start the engine. 'You

must tell the police, though,' he insisted. 'They've been looking for her all night – or should have been. It's only fair to let them know. Or shall I do it?'

'No, no, I'll do it,' said Fanny hastily. 'You just go. Leave it all to me.'

'I suppose it's all right.' Gordon was looking very worried. 'I don't even know what your name is.'

'Fanny Anthony.'

'Oh, yes.' His face cleared slightly. 'I've heard Bobbie mention you. Your father is a doctor, isn't he?'

'That's right. Now do *go*.' What the hell difference did it make *what* her father did? How *prejudiced* people were!

Gordon started his engine. Then a new thought struck him. 'Christ, you're supposed to be at school, aren't you? You can't possibly look after Bobbie!'

'I'm not supposed to be anywhere,' said Fanny masterfully, 'but you bloody well are. So why don't you go and do your bit, and I'll do mine!'

Gordon's face registered affronted dignity but collapsed into a grin. 'Cheeky piece!' he said. 'But thanks all the same. See you around.'

'See you.' Fanny waved cheerfully as he drove away. Then she thrust her hands into her pockets and thought hard. It was no good ringing up Bobbie. You couldn't tell someone over the phone that their father was dead. And she needed to get to her quickly, before Gordon decided to ring the police himself. It would be even worse if some ham-fisted policeman told her. 'Did you know, Miss, that while you've been gallivanting about causing people all this trouble, your father was dying?' Unthinkable. No, Fanny must somehow reach Bobbie first. So she needed a car and a helpful, sympathetic driver. This was where Stewart came in. Or Helen. Or even both. At once, before they started on the day's work.

Fanny went into the station and saw to her dismay that the telephone box had a woman inside it, leaning against the glass and clearly enjoying a long chat. What's more, a man was waiting by its door, glancing impatiently at his watch. There was only one thing to do. Fanny ran out of the station and approached a taxi which was standing on the rank.

'Overton Lodge, please,' she said. 'That's Dr Anthony's surgery, down the far end of Wilmot Road. And please be quick. It's extremely important.'

Only when the taxi had pulled out of the station yard in a fast curve did Fanny realise that she had left her plastic bag full of school books in Gordon's car.

That morning Mary Ross went singing into the bathroom, twirling her sponge bag cheerfully. She had tied her hair up in a spotted cotton scarf whose perky ends stuck up jauntily. There was a touch of the Hollywood nineteen-forties about the way she felt this morning, slightly dissipated and wildly attractive – a sort of *On The Town* feeling. What a *sweet* man Ken was! It seemed as if she had known him for years and years. 'In a previous existence, my love,' he had said, 'who knows? We have walked in a Tudor garden or trod the marble of the pyramids.' And then, with his self-mocking smile, he had added, 'Nothing like your Olliphant for instant poesie.'

It had been nearly two in the morning before Ken had left, creaking nervously down the stairs. 'Mis-spending my advancing years,' he whispered sibilantly, 'not to mention my youth.' But at the front door he had abandoned all jocularity. 'I'm forty-six, Mary,' he told her. 'Married twice, three kids, up to the neck in alimony. Just the kind of man your mother wouldn't want you to know. Honestly, you ought to tell me to bugger off. I haven't the masochism to do it myself.'

'My mother,' Mary had said, 'would simply adore you. She yearns for the Bohemian life, you see. Wanted to go on the stage but fetched up as a respectable headmaster's wife and all that's left of her ambitions is a rather Edith Evans voice and a tendency towards chiffon scarves.' And Ken had smiled a little sadly and said, 'She sounds a lovely lady.' Then he had kissed Mary again and suddenly, almost angrily, started down the steps, turning to say, 'Don't let me muck you about, Mary, for God's sake.' And Mary had simply laughed.

She smiled again now as she shut the door and bolted it, put her money in the meter, lit the geyser and turned on its tap. She was much braver now about the geyser's inevitable bang and it would save time if she brushed her teeth while the water was running in. She unscrewed the lid from her toothpaste and squeezed a little on to her brush. Goodness, that geyser *did* smell gassy this morning. Perhaps she should....

The force of the explosion blew the bathroom door off its hinges, shattered the window and brought down most of the ceiling. Lee Haynes, in pyjamas and slippers, rushed down from his room to see what had happened. Crunching over broken glass, he peered in, half afraid of a second explosion, since there was still a strong smell of gas. Nothing remained of the geyser except its tin coolie hat, which hung at a drunken angle from its pipe. Wisps of curtain hung in the empty window frame and the floor was thickly covered with plaster and scraps of metal and broken glass. Mary, Lee saw to his horror, lay motionless, her head obscured by a large piece of the geyser's casing. The fear of what he was going to find made Lee's stomach heave but he crunched across the floor and lifted off the piece of casing.

To his immense relief, Mary was intact. He squatted down beside her, trying to see if she was breathing. A deep cut on her shoulder was oozing blood. He felt her wrist clumsily, trying to remember which side of the bones the artery was. In case of electric shock, cover with a blanket. How did artificial respiration go? Why the hell hadn't he been on a first aid course? All this filthy plaster and stuff all over her – should he brush it off or might he cause more damage? Lee began to feel panicky.

'What is it, what has happened?' Mrs Mallalieu, still buttoning up her dressing gown, appeared in the doorway and the other tenants gathered behind her, staring with shocked faces into the bathroom. Lee looked up. 'Get a doctor for Christ's sake,' he said.

Mrs Mallalieu gave a little scream and rushed back to her room where there was the only telephone in the house. 'We ought to cover her up,' said Lee. 'Somebody get a blanket.' He felt better now that the others were there. He picked some of the larger pieces of rubble off Mary and pulled the edges of her housecoat together in an effort to keep her warm. As he did so, he saw that there was a pulse beating in her neck. He stood up. 'She's alive,' he said – and sat down, rather abruptly, on the edge of the bath, which had miraculously remained intact.

There was a babble of conflicting advice as people crunched across the littered floor with blankets and a pillow, Kleenex, a tin of Elastoplast, a glass of water and, from Miss Percy who lived in the garden flat, a cut-glass bottle of smelling salts. Mrs Mallalieu reappeared.

'I rang Dr Anthony,' she said. 'I don't know who Miss Ross has, but he's always very nice. Oh, my goodness.' She surveyed the devastation as frosty morning air blew in through the empty window frame. 'Whatever did the silly girl do to my geyser? It always worked so well, ever since my husband had it installed. Thank goodness I'm insured.'

Mary became aware, first dimly and then acutely, of a violent pain in her head. Difficult to understand, waking up with such a pain. Difficult to wake up.

With a great struggle, she managed to connect her mind to the mechanism which opened her eyes. A blast of blinding light drove in, causing an agonised, soundless buzzing somewhere in her brain. She flinched away from the painful effort, uttering a faint sound of protest.

'Mary,' said a man's voice, very near to her, 'it's all right. Just keep still. You'll be fine.'

Mary slid away into oblivion again but, after a timeless interval, found herself more strongly conscious. A faint curiosity ran through her and she gathered her strength for some minutes and then opened her eyes. The pain was still intense and she found that she could see two overlapping, transparent images of everything. Twin mis-registered lampshades, flowered curtains over other flowered curtains, table across table, floated past her vision and then, fleshlessly duplicated but oddly reassuring, came the faces of someone familiar.

'There you are!' said the faces kindly. And then they

turned away to present their ghostly profiles. 'She's come to, nurse!' they said.

Mary felt extremely puzzled but the mechanics of conveying her perplexity were exhaustingly complicated. Since looking was easier than talking, she summoned all her energy for the task of understanding the floating, overlapping faces. After what seemed a long period of fruitless hard work, she suddenly understood that she was in a room which was not her own and that the faces belonged to Lee Haynes. How very odd.

'That's a girl!' said Lee cheerily. 'Hey, you made a good job of that bathroom – Mrs Mallalieu is tickled to death. She'll get the whole job done on the insurance now!'

'Ssh,' said another voice, a female one this time. 'Don't try to make her talk.' This voice seemed to belong to a pair of faces in white caps. Mary closed her eyes again. It was all too much to understand.

'Helen, can I have thirty-five pence for a taxi, please? He's waiting outside. I'll explain why, but do be quick.'

'Right.' Helen fished stoically in her purse. 'Matthew, give this to the man, will you?'

'That's more than thirty-five,' said Matthew, inspecting the coins.

'You have to tip taxi drivers.'

'Why do you?'

'Oh, just *go*, Matthew!' Fanny exploded. 'Helen, is Stewart here?'

'No, he went out some time ago on an urgent call – some girl over in Farringdon Hill blew up a geyser. Now, Fanny, what *is* going on? Have you found Bobbie?'

'Almost. Look.' Fanny thrust the crumpled note at Helen. 'This was in her letter box and I was just going round to the Brethren when someone called Gordon arrived in a car. He's Marjorie's husband – that's Bobbie's elder sister – and he said Bobbie's father died last night. Isn't it awful? She doesn't know, you see, so I want to find her and tell her before the police do.'

'Heavens. Look, there's a lot more I want to know about all this but we'll go and get Bobbie first. Where is she?'

'Probably at home by now. We knocked up the Brethren but they said she wasn't there. It was a funny girl like the Angel Gabriel.' Fanny gave a little giggle then added, 'Poor Bobbie, though. It's so awful for her.'

Helen was pushing her arms into her suède coat. 'Now, you boys are all right, aren't you? Did you deal with the taxi driver, Matthew?'

'Yes. He just took the money and went. Do they always do that?'

'Mostly, yes. Just finish your breakfast and get yourselves off to school. OK?'

'Can I have drinking chocolate on my cornflakes?' asked Dominic.

'Yes. Come on, Fanny.'

As Helen was backing the car out of the garage, Fanny said, 'There's the Brethren's ambulance.'

'Ambulance?'

'That psychedelic thing. Wonder where they're off to. You don't suppose Bobbie's a prisoner inside it, do you, being made the victim of some weird rite?'

'I think Bobbie's got far too much sense to be made anyone's prisoner. As to the rites, I simply can't start to imagine what goes on with these people. There are some sects which make quite absurd rules so as not to interfere with God's will.'

'Oh, I don't think they're like that,' said Fanny. 'They're not a bit authoritarian. They all look terribly gentle and relaxed.'

'Ridiculous.'

'Why?'

'Nobody can be gentle and relaxed in this day and age. Willy-nilly, we're thrown into a competitive society and the only way you can opt out of the business of surviving is to get someone else to do it for you. Sponge, in fact.'

'Well, I think it would be awfully boring, just living simply and praising the Lord, but I don't see why they shouldn't, if that's what turns them on.'

'Oh dear,' said Helen, 'I'm going to be lectured about tolerance again.'

Fanny laughed. 'No, you're not. I'll let you off this morning.'

'Thank you,' said Helen – and Fanny laughed again at her mother's unsuccessful attempt to sound meek.

Bobbie's house, to Fanny's intense disappointment, was as unresponsive as before. She rang the bell and banged savagely on the knocker for the third time and then, mocked by the silence, went slowly back to the little Fiat.

'No?' asked Helen.

'No. But where *is* she, then?'

'She must still be with those funny people, after all. Who did you see this morning, exactly? Was it anyone trustworthy?'

'A small child first, and then this Biblical-looking girl. Ruth, the child called her. She seemed quite straightforward – she even asked us in to look.'

'And did you go in?'

'No, because Gordon had to go and fetch Marjorie and Mrs Rippon from the hospital.'

'H'm. Then *I'll* go in,' said Helen, letting in the clutch.

Outside the brick building where the Brethren lived, two police cars and a riot van stood with their blue lights flashing. The painted ambulance was drawn up by the wall, its rear doors open. Gideon, Amos, Paul and Ezekiel were lined up beside it, surrounded by policemen while Ruth argued with more policemen at the doorway of the building, Jeremiah at her side. A rapidly increasing crowd was collecting but there was no sign of Bobbie.

Fanny leapt out of the Fiat almost before Helen had stopped it. She rushed across the road to the group at the door and shouted, 'Where's Bobbie? I've *got* to see her!'

'She is indoors,' said Ruth in her rich, calm, Californian voice. 'And she is very upset. You must all leave her alone to make her peace with God and see her way clearly. I promised her she is safe with us in the Lord and I shall keep that promise. Amen.'

'I hope you realise, miss,' said one of the policemen to Ruth, 'that you are guilty of obstructing the police in the course of their duty. We have reason to believe that you are holding this girl against her will. There are very severe penalties.'

'They're kidnappers!' screamed a woman in the crowd. 'They lure kids away from their homes. We all know they do!'

'Bloody long-haired layabouts,' a man chipped in. 'You want to get in there, mate,' he added to the policemen. There was a general mutter of agreement from the crowd. They were pressing in more closely, almost leaning against the policemen surrounding the boys by the ambulance.

'Look, miss, if you'll just let us in, we can talk this over more privately,' said the policeman to Ruth. 'Come on, now. This is getting to be a nasty situation and you're making it worse.'

Jeremiah suddenly burst out, 'Why don't you leave us alone? Everywhere we go it's the same. You come and accuse us of taking drugs or stealing things or abducting people's children and so we lose our home because you get the landlord to turn us out. Well, this time you're not coming in here. This is our home and we're staying in it. We've done no harm.'

'We can use force,' said the policeman.

Fanny felt a powerful jostling in the crowd beside her and, turning, saw that her mother was thrusting her way between the people.

'What's going on?' inquired Helen.

'Bobbie's inside,' said Fanny, 'but they won't let the police in.' She leaned forward, trying to speak directly to Ruth. 'Listen,' she said, 'I'm Bobbie's friend. She'll want to see me. Tell her it's Fanny. Please!'

Ruth cast a brief glance at Fanny, who looked neat and unremarkable in her school uniform, backed by her suède-coated mother, and shook her head. It was evident that she classed them as part of the forces of invasion.

Fanny tried one last, desperate shot. 'Listen – Bobbie's father died last night,' she said. 'Does she know?'

Ruth's face did not change as she continued to confront her

enemies. With her chin up and her fists planted defiantly on her hips she stared resolutely at the policeman who most directly threatened her. 'Yes,' she said absently in answer to Fanny's question, 'she knows.' But she did not shift her gaze from the policeman's face.

They had wrapped Bobbie in a blanket on top of all her other clothes because she could not stop shivering. The iron flap of the coke stove in the kitchen was open and its red glow scorched her leg through a gap in the blanket but she made no move to avoid its heat. She sat very deep in a brown rexine armchair which had broken springs so that her knees were level with her chest and this gave her, she noticed absently, a faint feeling of ludicrous indignity. It was an odd thing to be aware of, because nothing mattered any more. Nothing would ever matter again. Her hands were clamped round a mug of tea and her whole body felt rigid, as if it had been poured into a mould and had set there as solid as concrete, except that from time to time a violent shudder passed through her. She would crack and fall into pieces, she thought compassionately, gazing down from some detached dream place at her poor, stiff body sitting in the arm chair.

The Brethren stood grouped round Bobbie, murmuring concernedly among themselves. Ruth knelt on the floor beside the brown armchair, resting her clasped hands on its arm as she talked in a quiet, unceasing monotone.

'It seems bad now, it seems the Lord has done a bad thing in taking your father from you, a thing that no one can understand. But the Lord knows us, Bobbie, he knows us better than we know ourselves, he made us and we are his children. You are not alone, Bobbie, your father in Heaven loves you and cares for you. . . .'

Unhearing, Bobbie stared into the red glow of the coke fire while the haunting sequence of dreadful pictures happened again and again. The terrible thing was that she had been so happy. He was dying and she had been happy, crowded in the ambulance with Gideon and the others, eating oranges and singing. It had sounded lovely, the singing, with the boys doing their Deep River harmony and everyone clapping the rhythm and Bobbie's voice clear and sweet, oh, how wicked to love the sound of her own voice. 'Great!' they said. 'That's great!' And she picked up all the orange peel because she wanted to look after them, her new big brothers, and she was still holding it when they came singing back home and Gideon opened the ambulance door and the police were there. Jeremiah had shouted something from the driver's seat but, singing, they hadn't heard him.

The policewoman with the round pink face was there specially for Bobbie, she knew that, they always have women if they have to arrest a girl and Bobbie's hands were full of orange peel so she couldn't get out of the van easily. The policewoman helped her down although she had this pink face that looked like a doll and she still held Bobbie's arm quite tightly as they walked across to the door where Ruth was standing, not letting anyone in.

Why is she taking me to the door, thought Bobbie, she can arrest me here, she's brought policemen with her and a van with a blue light on top, she can arrest me here.

But she still hadn't thought there was anything else.

'Is your name Roberta Rippon?'

Shirley Temple, Donald Duck, Fanny Anthony. 'Yes.'

'I'm afraid I have some bad news for you. Can we go inside?'

Bad news, is that what they called arresting people, bad news?

Ruth stood like stone in the doorway, statue still. 'No, you may not come in.' The policewoman's face puckered with worry. 'I want to speak to Roberta in private.'

'There are no secrets between sisters in God,' Ruth told her. 'Say what you have to say.'

Long corridors, locked cells, wire mesh across the stair well. Bobbie found herself shuddering.

The policewoman seemed embarrassed. 'Listen, my dear,' she began – and then noticed the orange peel in Bobbie's hands. 'Somebody find a bin, for goodness' sake,' she said irritably. One of the policemen came up with a cardboard box, dark brown at the bottom because it was wet, and Bobbie dropped the orange peel into it. Her hands were sticky.

'It's about your father,' said the policewoman.

'My father?' Not prison.

'You know he was in hospital?'

'Yes.'

'I'm very sorry to have to tell you this, my dear, but – well, his injuries were very much worse than anyone thought. He – I'm afraid he died this morning.'

No. No – no – no – no – no.

'I'm so sorry,' the policewoman said.

Not real. Not true.

There was jostling then, as the policewoman made to lead Bobbie across to the waiting car, but Ruth was quicker. She was at Bobbie's side before anyone realised that she had left her post at the door and, with an arm closely round Bobbie's shoulders, she guided her through a protecting crowd of the Brethren to the haven of the brick building.

'Roberta must go to her mother!' insisted the policewoman.

'Later,' said Ruth, resuming her stance at the door. And Bobbie was gently fussed into the low armchair before the coke stove, wrapped in a blanket and given a cup of tea, hugged and kissed and prayed for until her weeping gave way to a dry, convulsive shuddering.

Bobbie stared at the glowing coke. Singing, she had let him die. No. This was not quite final, it couldn't be. It was a dream, another of the nightmarish dreams, and nothing had happened yet to wake her from it.

Fair-haired Gideon was on his knees beside her, his eyes troubled behind his wire-rimmed spectacles.

'Try to believe,' he urged gently. 'Faith can take away all pain. Your father is with God, Bobbie – he is one with the Lord, he is with you and in you for ever.'

Unwillingly, Bobbie heard him. His words were meant as comfort and yet they ended all hope.

She put her hands over her face, blindly seeking the small comfort of the touch of her own body, and smelt the bitter, oily reek of orange peel. And then she knew that it was true.

There was no escape from this terrible reality. There was no defence against the pain of it and, even in the deepest centre of her mind, there was no refuge.

'Ah, Fanny.' Miss Beacon took off her glasses and smiled. 'Do sit down.'

Suspiciously, Fanny sat down. Why the bonhomie? Clearly she had been summoned here for a telling-off about being late for school this morning. Helen had dropped her off, after Bobbie had disappeared into the old warehouse with Ruth.

'Now, I do want you to feel that this is a completely informal little talk,' went on Miss Beacon, 'and it goes without saying, of course, that anything you can tell me will be completely confidential.'

Will be taken down in writing and may be used as evidence, Fanny thought. Miss Beacon was still talking.

'... and I do, naturally, regard loyalty to friends as a very basic and natural human feeling. But there are times when a situation crops up which may require unusual measures to deal with it. Now, I believe that such a situation has occurred regarding one of the girls in your class, Roberta Rippon.' She paused, but Fanny said nothing. 'I'm sure you understand, Fanny, how very important it is for us to find out where Roberta is.' Another pause.

'Why?' said Fanny suddenly.

'Why?' Miss Beacon raised pained eyebrows. 'I should have thought it was obvious. She may be in quite grave danger. She may be with totally irresponsible people or she may even have had some kind of accident. What I want to know is, did Roberta confide any plans to you, Fanny?'

'No,' said Fanny, relieved that she could answer honestly.

Miss Beacon refrained from sighing. 'Well, perhaps you can help me in a different way, then. Have you any idea why Roberta rushed out of school in the violent way she did? She actually slammed the door behind her so hard that she smashed the window, did you know that?'

'No,' said Fanny.

'Is she not happy at school?' Miss Beacon prodded insistently. 'Is there anything we should know which would help her and help us?'

Fanny shook her head, paralysed with caution. The woman was asking her, in effect, to tell her all about Bobbie. What it was like to *be* Bobbie.

Miss Beacon, observing Fanny's dilemma, had the sense to remain silent. At last Fanny was forced to speak.

'I don't know about *happy*,' she said reluctantly, taking what seemed to be a reasonably harmless point. 'I mean, some people just *aren't* very happy, are they?'

Miss Beacon looked interested.

'I mean,' Fanny blundered on, 'it seems so stupid to think that everyone is happy at school and if someone isn't, then there must be something wrong. The way schools are, it seems quite natural that lots of people aren't happy. It's not a question of happiness being "normal", like an exam pass mark.'

'We're talking about Roberta,' Miss Beacon reminded her. 'Is *Roberta* happy?'

'She isn't tough enough to be happy,' said Fanny, irritated. 'She really worries about school – whether she's got things right, whether she's going to get into a row. But she likes it. She likes it better than home, really. It's just that school – this kind of school, anyway – makes it so important to be a winner. Nobody's interested in what you are, only in what you do. It doesn't matter so much to people like me, because I don't care all that much. But Bobbie *cares*.'

'I can't say I find that a bad thing,' said Miss Beacon.

'No, but there are alternatives,' Fanny insisted. 'I mean, if we all suddenly thought one day, "I don't believe in education" and decided not to come – all over the country, I mean, *all* of us – then there'd *have* to be a new system.'

Miss Beacon looked up from her blotter where she had written a note. 'Perhaps you would like to put your views to the school Debating Society,' she suggested drily. 'Thank you, Fanny, you've been most helpful.'

Oh, she was adroit, the old bitch, Fanny reflected bitterly. She knew how to keep her head and make you lose yours. And when she'd had enough, you *knew* she'd had enough.

'Feel free to come and see me at any time, won't you?' Miss Beacon continued as Fanny stood up.

'Yes,' said Fanny. And then, although cursing herself for a renegade, she added, 'Thank you.'

'Just one more thing,' said Miss Beacon. 'Miss Perkins would like to see you at break. You won't forget, will you?'

'No,' said Fanny.

As the door closed, Miss Beacon leaned back in her chair and looked at the note she had written on her blotter, tapping her teeth thoughtfully with her Biro. It read, 'Rippon "likes school better than home" (F.A.) Why?'

Following her interview with Miss Beacon, Fanny went down to the clammy comfort of Cloakroom D. See Miss Perkins at break, indeed! Not likely. There would be a fearful row about the missing bag of books left in Gordon's car and about the continued absence of her hat, and she would have to make some sort of explanation about being late this morning, but if possible without mentioning Bobbie. The Beacon bird was bad enough, but you couldn't talk about *anything* personal with Miss Perkins. She was just a desiccated discipline machine.

Fanny sighed. What a waste of time it was, being at school when there was so much to do! It was mean of Helen to insist on leaving Bobbie to the police. Just because they'd been too late to break the bad news to her, it didn't mean the poor girl didn't need a bit of looking after.

Fanny stared at her reflection in the mirror on the cream-painted brick wall. At break time it was always surrounded by a jostling crowd of hair-combing girls and so, celebrating the luxury of having her reflection all to herself, Fanny gazed closely at her image. Her early morning effort at make-up had been a bit sketchy and the bag which she had left in Gordon's car contained her little make-up case. Never mind. All was not lost. Fanny's shoe bag contained a few stand-by cosmetics.

Fanny applied a grey eye shadow, followed by a little white gloss on the upper lids. She brushed her lashes with mascara and painted a thin dark line along the extreme edge of both eyelids. There. Beautiful. She gave herself a critical stare. Left to itself, Fanny's face was, she knew, not striking. It was pretty enough but slightly amorphous, grey-eyed and brown-haired and depressingly young.

There had been rows at first over her insistence on wearing make-up at school and angry notes were sent home, to Stewart's amusement and Helen's annoyance. Fanny had soon found, though, that the trick was to arrive wearing a surplus quantity of brightly-coloured eye shadow which she obediently removed on request. After a few days of this, she turned up wearing her normal make-up which occasioned no comment, and had continued to do so ever since.

She packed her things back into the shoe bag then, as an afterthought, got out a tiny tin of colourless antiseptic cream (free sample to doctors) and applied some to her lips. Marvellous stuff this. It served the dual purpose of glamorising the lips and preventing them from chapping and was absolutely essential for anyone about to venture out into the cold. Which Fanny was. She put on her gabardine mac and went out of the cloakroom door with its newly-mended window. She walked without hurry down the tarmac path to the gate. As she turned into the road, she glanced at her watch – an artistic touch, she thought, guaranteed to convince anyone watching that she was making sure that she was not late for a dental appointment. She was glad, however, that Miss Beacon's office was screened from the pavement by a tall, thick laurel hedge, for the way to the Brethren made it necessary for Fanny to walk past the Headmistress's window. And she had no desire for a second interview with Miss Beacon in such a short space of time.

Miss Beacon, however, was not in her office. Following her encounter with Fanny, she had found herself, unusually, in a state of slight uncertainty. She was, in principle, firmly wedded to the concept of the pyramid structure, seeing her school as a roughly triangular shape with the youngest and least significant children forming the broad base and herself at the top. Today she toyed unnervingly with the idea that she presided over a volcano rather than a pyramid.

These modern children whose parents had allowed them to rely far too much on their own inadequately-based judgement, the iconoclasts, the doubting kind, were an enemy to themselves as well as to everyone else.

Irritably, Miss Beacon had left her office for a therapeutic walk round the school. She had always found the routine hum of voices and the sight of industriously bent heads soothing at moments of stress, and this occasion was no exception. She was in a far more composed state of mind as she passed the gothic window at the turn of the library stairs. Glancing out, her eye was caught by the sight of a girl outside on the pavement, walking calmly past the laurel hedge. She looked more closely and saw that it was Fanny Anthony.

For a moment, Miss Beacon felt furiously angry. How dare the wretched girl flout authority in this way? She stared at Fanny's retreating back. Where did she think she was off to? The question answered itself almost at once. Of course, Fanny would be going to try and find Roberta Rippon. Miss Beacon sighed. There was going to be a lot trouble about that.

There was a sound of pattering footsteps and Miss Beacon turned to see their cause. The school secretary, Mrs Williams, was scampering up the stairs towards her. 'Oh, Miss Beacon,' she said breathlessly, 'it's the police on the phone. They want to speak to you – they say they've got some news about Roberta Rippon.'

Gordon drove his car grimly through the undemanding midday traffic of south London, wondering how long it would take his newly widowed mother-in-law to stop crying. She sat beside him, ludicrous in the pink suit she had worn last night when they were summoned to the hospital. 'I'm sure it'll cheer him up,' she had said. 'I bought it when he took me to Wimbledon last year and he adored it.' And now she sat, pink-suited and pink-nosed, with tears coursing effortlessly down her face. She touched her eyes occasionally with a tiny, sodden hanky but it was a useless gesture.

Marjorie, in the back seat with her head obstinately in the

middle of Gordon's driving mirror, had at intervals offered Kleenex, a Polo mint and a Valium tablet but had met with no response except for a tiny movement of the head from side to side.

'I expect Bobbie'll be at home by the time we get there,' said Gordon cheerfully. 'That'll be nice. The old cops are jolly good, aren't they, keeping us in the picture. That message at the hospital was quite a relief. I was pretty frantic this morning, I can tell you, when that Virgin Mary girl said Bobbie wasn't there.'

'You *must* have been,' said Marjorie loyally.

'I thought afterwards,' Gordon ploughed on, 'that it might be silly to leave it to Fanny to ring the cops. They might think it was a bit – well – irresponsible. And of course, she wouldn't have thought to tell them which hospital we were at. We wouldn't have got the message.'

'I think you were very sensible,' said Marjorie. 'What a funny thing for her to do, though, spending the night at a place like that. Did she know them before, do you think? Had she been in the habit of going there?'

'No idea,' said Gordon. 'Do you know, Mum?'

Sylvia moved her head very slowly from side to side.

'What you need,' said Gordon compassionately, 'is a good stiff drink.'

Sylvia whirled round in her seat, her hands clenched in quivering fists.

'Don't say that to me! I'm not an alcoholic, I'm not! That's what *he* always said and it isn't true, it never was! I tried to explain but he wouldn't listen – he *needn't* have died, Gordon! It was all such a silly mistake and he went flaring off – he *needn't* have died.'

Gordon's initial alarm gave way to admiration. Old Sylvia was taking it on the chin, then.

He slowed a little for a distant traffic light although it stood at green, and was gratified to see it change to amber and then to red. One develops an instinct for these things, he told himself as he brought the car unhurriedly to a halt. A sort of finer intuition. Poor old David never had it.

Sylvia was sobbing angrily now, her inadequate handkerchief pressed to her nose. Still weeping, she stretched a hand behind her to Marjorie and clicked her fingers. Marjorie obediently gave her a Kleenex and said, 'Mum, I honestly do think you'd find a Valium a great help. They're not habit-forming, you know.'

'Shut up,' said Sylvia.

'There goes another *Lord of the Rings*,' said Helen to Colin with satisfaction as the bookshop door closed behind a customer. 'I've always said that children like a good solid book. There's so much *froth* on the market these days.'

'M'm,' said Colin absentmindedly. He put one finger on the corner of a publisher's poster which had come loose from the wall and pressed it for some seconds. When he removed his finger it sprang loose again.

'What d'you mean, "M'm"?' demanded Helen. 'I thought you were all in favour of froth, Colin. You're always going on about Visual Appeal. You're a bit of a zombie this morning.'

'Sorry.'

'What's the matter?'

'Nothing.'

'Look, don't let's be silly about this. Have I *said* anything?'

'No, of course not. It's nothing.'

'Colin.' Helen sat down on the table in the Story Corner and pulled out a chair for Colin. 'I'm sorry to be a bore, but for goodness' sake – look, something's cropped up, hasn't it? You've been mooning round here like a sleepwalker all morning. Do you want the day off so you can deal with it, whatever it is? I can manage, you know.'

'No, I wouldn't dream of it.' Colin was slightly shocked by her generosity.

'Then what's the *matter*?' Helen shouted this question and Colin turned very red with annoyance.

'It's Bobbie, if you must know,' he said angrily. 'You come in here and tell me she spent the night with some gang of cranky freaks and this morning she's been told that her father's dead and then you expect me to converse intelligently about the work of Tolkien.'

'Oh, Colin, I'm so sorry.' Helen put her hand contritely on Colin's knee and, when he glared at it belligerently, took it off again. 'What a clumsy fool I am. I'd no idea that Bobbie meant anything to you or I'd never have poured out that story as if it was just any old domestic drama.'

'What would you have said, then? "Colin, dear, I'm afraid there's bad news about your girlfriend"?'

'Yes,' said Helen simply.

There was a pause and then Colin laughed, relaxing in his child-sized, pale blue painted chair.

'I'm sorry,' he said. 'It's not your fault. Of course it's not. Bobbie's so – well, so vulnerable, somehow. She makes me feel as if I don't want to let her out of my sight. And it's crazy because I've only met her once – apart from the times before, when I hadn't noticed her.'

'I'm glad you feel like that. I mean, I'm glad *somebody* does. I don't know Bobbie all that well but she comes to the house quite a bit and I think she has a rather tough time of it at home. I never met her father but I gather he was some kind of high-powered executive who was never there. And her mother – well!'

'What d'you mean?' inquired Colin cautiously.

'She's so temperamental! Fanny swears she's an alcoholic but you know how Fanny exaggerates. I took Bobbie home one night though, a bit late – we'd all been watching something good on television and you know how time slips by – and I dropped her at the gate and was just driving off when I heard her mother screaming at her like a fishwife. So I switched off the engine and marched up the path and introduced myself.'

Colin grinned. 'I can imagine. What did she say?'

'Oh, she went all queenly. Asked me in and poured me the biggest gin and tonic I've ever seen and wanted to know if I played bridge. And then she started on about children. "They ruin one's whole life," she said. "Don't you agree? When I think of what I could have *been*...." Sort of implying that she might have run the Civil Service or been a Grand Prix racing driver. A complete fantasist.'

'*Do* you play bridge?' inquired Colin.

'Oh, no! Can you imagine me getting involved in a bitchy little debate about whether I could have finessed a Jack or something?'

'You sound as if you know about it.'

'Well ...' Helen was defensive, 'my mother used to play. She insisted on teaching me the rudiments. It is the *only* card game, of course, but oh God, what a waste of time!'

'My dad plays cribbage,' said Colin. 'In the pub with his mates.'

'It's no use, Colin,' said Helen firmly, 'you are not going to make me feel guilty about my privileged upbringing. Now look, take the afternoon off and go round to that dotty place and see if you can see Bobbie. Or if the police have taken her home, go round there. She's probably longing to see you.'

'D'you really think so?' Colin's face lit up for a moment and then he returned to gravity. 'I tell you what,' he said with his scrupulous Scottish fair-mindedness, 'I'll take a bit longer at lunch time and try to see her then. But I'll be back by half past three when the kids start coming out of school. We're always busy then.'

'Right,' said Helen, 'but if you get involved, don't bother coming back. I'll understand.'

Colin grinned. 'Oh, the courtesy of it all!' he said. 'We're getting too bloody virtuous to breathe!'

'In that case,' said Helen crisply, 'I suggest that you get a damp cloth and wipe the shelves in the Toddlers' Corner. Someone has made a nasty mess with a sticky lolly. A nice, *rude* job for you.'

'I should have kept my great trap shut,' said Colin.

Fanny wished that she could have changed out of her school clothes. It was impossible to be taken seriously when garbed in an absurd uniform devised eighty years ago. There was a Comic Cuts element about it which reduced everyone who wore it to the status of a garden gnome.

As she approached the place where the Brethren lived, Fanny passed a police car, stationary at the kerb side. The two policemen sitting in it looked bored but they both sat up when they saw Fanny, and watched her attentively as she walked ahead of them towards the warehouse door. Fanny was acutely aware of them. Consciously, she slowed her pace and relaxed her shoulders, thinking herself into the part of a schoolgirl on a legitimate outing. She turned off the pavement at the last moment to approach the warehouse door and raised her hand to rap on it with her knuckles. Then, remembering Ruth's steadfast refusal to admit anyone that morning, she changed her mind and gave the door a tentative push. It did not budge. Frustrated, and aware of the police car's slow progress along the kerb towards her, Fanny gave it a furious shove. To her surprise, the door yielded at once to this assault, having been held only on a click fitting like a cupboard, its Yale lock snibbed back. Fanny went inside quickly, closing the door behind her. The hall-like room was empty except for its dozens of wooden chairs but she heard a murmur of voices from a room at the far end whose door stood open. She crossed the big room quietly and looked round the door.

Bobbie, huddled in a blanket, sat deep in an armchair which was pulled close to a glowing red stove. Her face was pink from the stove's heat as she stared unblinkingly into the flames. She looked very small. Several of the Brethren stood near by, cutting up vegetables on a large deal table. One of them, a dark, bearded boy with blue eyes, looked up and saw Fanny.

'Hey,' he said, 'someone's come in. Look.'

Ruth looked up, her hands arrested in the action of peeling a parsnip. 'What do you want?' she asked.

'I've come for Bobbie,' said Fanny.

'Fanny! Oh, Fanny, Fanny!'

Bobbie struggled up from the armchair and out of the enveloping folds of blanket and began to run across to Fanny but her legs, half-paralysed by the cramped uncounted hours she had spent in the sagging chair, gave way under her and she pitched headlong on to the floor. 'Fanny!' Tears poured down her face.

'It's all right, Bobbie. There, don't cry.' Fanny felt a lump swell in her own throat as she helped Bobbie into a sitting position on the floor and put her arm round her. After a little time, when Bobbie's sobbing had slackened to a series of gasping exhausted breaths, she said, 'Listen, lovey, what shall we do? Do you want to stay here?'

Bobbie shook her head.

'Would you like to come to my house?'

This suggestion seemed to bring confusion and a suggestion of fresh tears.

'You want to go home, don't you.' Fanny was not asking a question. 'Come on. Upsy daisy.' Ruth and Gideon came forward to help Bobbie to her feet but Fanny put out a defensive hand.

'Please,' said Ruth, 'we only want to help you. If our sister cannot find comfort among us then the Lord will care for her in another way.'

Bobbie stood up a little unsteadily and looked round at Fanny and at the Brethren. Her face was grotesquely swollen with weeping but Fanny was relieved to see that her unfocused look had gone. 'You've been very kind,' she said huskily. 'I'd like to stay, in a way. But I don't believe the way you do. I can't. I wish I could '

'Come on,' said Fanny quickly. 'Home's the place for you. Have you got a coat or anything?'

Bobbie shook her head and Fanny took her by the arm, impelling her gently towards the door. 'This is a funny woolly you're wearing,' she said, 'this green thing. Never seen that before.' As she reached the door which led into the big room, Fanny felt a hand on her shoulder. Turning violently to face her assailant, Fanny found herself confronted by a policewoman.

'Please don't be alarmed,' said the policewoman. 'We're here to help you.'

Two policemen stood at the far side of the room and Jeremiah clenched his fists with anger at the sight of them. 'I *told* you we should have locked the door!' he shouted at Ruth.

'This is the Lord's house,' said Ruth implacably, 'and those who wish to come to us will find a way. The door is on the click. Only our enemies will find it locked.'

'You're right there, Miss,' agreed one of the policemen, grinning. 'It wasn't until the young lady here pushed it open that we realised it wasn't locked.'

Ruth ignored him. 'What are you going to do with Bobbie?' she asked the policewoman, but before she could answer Bobbie herself said tiredly, 'She has come to arrest me, of course.'

The injustice of this suggestion made the policewoman's round face turn brightly pink. 'That's nonsense!' she said indignantly. 'We just want to see you safely home, you silly girl! Your mother will be back by now and she'll be worried about you.'

'Well, I'm jolly glad you're here,' said Fanny, 'because it's a long walk from here to Bobbie's house. Can I come in the car, too?'

'Oh, please come, Fanny!' pleaded Bobbie.

'Of course she can come.' The policewoman was soothing and made no attempt to touch either Fanny or Bobbie as she walked beside them to the door but as they went outside Fanny could not help noticing that one of the policemen preceded them and the other fell in behind.

The police car reached Bobbie's house very quickly and the little procession of police-escorted girls walked up the path to the front door. Nobody ever answers that door, thought Fanny wildly, so it's no use you ringing the bell. This time, however, the door was flung open before they had even reached it and Marjorie, neat in a black dress and a plastic apron which said, 'Daddie's Favourite Sauce' ushered them into the house. She kissed Bobbie and said, 'Thank goodness you're back.' Gordon, hovering in the hall with a glass of gin in his hand, said, 'Would anyone like a drink?' And then, seeing that the party were either in police uniform or else below the legal drinking age, added, 'Oh. Perhaps not.'

'Where's Mum?' asked Bobbie.

'In the lounge.' Marjorie opened the door and Bobbie, very hesitantly, went in. She advanced towards her mother, who was standing by the French windows, aware that the door still stood open behind her and that the people in the hall were quiet, listening for some words of communication between Sylvia and herself.

'Mum—' she began.

'It's my fault,' said Sylvia in a strangled voice. 'All my fault. I know that.'

'It isn't!' Bobbie reached her mother and hugged her. 'Don't be silly.'

Sylvia began to cry. 'I am silly, aren't I? Oh, Bobbie, you're the only one who understands. My little Bobbie.'

Dry-eyed, Bobbie stroked her mother's hair.

The rhythmic stroking dimmed her own awareness to a point where she was conscious of little more than an immense weariness. The door into the room was shut gently from outside as Marjorie turned to face the little group in the hall. 'I think we'd better leave them together,' she said. 'They've always been very close. Would you like to go into the other room? I'm sure there are things to talk about.'

Unnoticed, Fanny slid round to stand beside Gordon, who seemed to be the only person not directly involved in Marjorie's shepherdings. He gave her a conspiratorial glance and whispered, 'Would you like a drink?'

'Yes, please,' said Fanny.

Gordon promptly led the way into the kitchen, where the mid-day sun reflected brightly from the unusually clean surfaces. 'Gin?'

'I like vodka and lime really, but I'll try anything.'

Gordon poured a large gin and tonic which Fanny sipped cautiously and found, to her relief, that she liked.

' "Very close." ' Gordon quoted his wife's words with irony. 'My God. Do you think they're very close?'

'I don't know. It's all a bit frightening, really.'

'What is?' Gordon drained his glass and poured himself another.

'All this emotion. I mean, you take it for granted that people love each other but when something like this happens, it seems so different. All demanding and destructive, somehow.'

43

'You're right there, kiddo. Cheers!'

'Cheers.' Fanny held out her glass to clink it against Gordon's, glad to be uninvolved in complex emotions, free and superior. As she drank, she stared coolly into Gordon's eyes, noticing them to be tawny brown, almost the colour of marmalade.

Gordon, staring back at Fanny, put his glass down steadily on the table. Then he took Fanny's glass from her hand and put it beside his own. Fanny knew that he was going to kiss her and felt a faint flutter of alarm which was in itself oddly enjoyable. Her next breath was filled with the smell of Gordon as he took her in his arms and pressed his mouth over hers. Although she did not like the slightly soapy fragrance its closeness was exciting and she put her arms round Gordon's neck. Then she detached herself.

'Hey,' said Gordon huskily, 'don't stop.'

Fanny gave a little laugh and picked up her drink but Gordon kissed her again, pressing himself strongly against her. 'You're lovely, aren't you,' he said. 'All female inside that white blouse. I bet you even wear a tie.'

'Not if I can help it,' said Fanny, disengaging herself again. 'It's rolled up in my mac pocket.' Her practicality deflated him and he sighed noisily, running his fingers through his hair.

'It shouldn't be allowed,' he said, 'or I shouldn't, or something.'

Marjorie's voice sounded from the hall. 'You've been most helpful and we really do appreciate it very much. Goodbye.'

The front door shut and Gordon had taken a couple of quick steps away from Fanny by the time Marjorie came into the kitchen and was leaning casually against the dishwasher.

'All gone, have they?' he greeted her.

'Yes, they have. I do think you might have come in, Gordon. I think they thought it was a bit funny.'

'You know me – I'm not much good at that sort of thing,' Gordon excused himself. 'And anyway, someone had to look after Fanny here, didn't they? If she hadn't gone barging into that nutty place Bobbie would still be there, wouldn't she?'

'Yes, we are really very indebted to you, Fanny,' Marjorie

said dutifully, glancing rather dubiously at the glass in Fanny's hand. 'What are you going to do now? Go back to school?'

'I suppose I'd better.'

'What about lunch? I'll be doing omelettes for Gordon and me – I don't know if Bobbie and Mum will feel like eating....'

'No, really, it's quite all right.' Fanny finished her gin.

'Are you sure you won't stay?' Marjorie had the kitchen door open and Fanny found herself walking through it.

'Hang on a tick,' said Gordon. 'You left a whole bagful of books in my car this morning – I'll come and get them out for you.'

'I'll start doing the omelettes, then,' said Marjorie, with a faint note of warning.

Outside at the car, Gordon handed Fanny her books.

'Here we are.' He sounded uneasy beneath the jocularity.

'Thank you.'

'I'd better not be too long.'

'No, your omelette will spoil.'

'You didn't mind?'

' 'Course not.'

'Great. Well – see you, then.'

'See you.'

Fanny set off down the street with a cheery wave to Gordon and walked briskly until she reached the turning into Wilmot Road. There she paused. What to do now? She felt irritable and let down. Bobbie was safely home and life suddenly seemed notably deficient in drama. The anticlimax of going back to school would be quite intolerable. What was it this afternoon? Double Latin, French. Oh, no. Not after police cars and mid-day gin and an almost-seduction. Thinking of Gordon, Fanny again felt a half-guilty surge of excitement. Perhaps, she thought, I am what Stewart calls a shameless hussy, but it really would be nice to go to bed with someone. Not Gordon, though. There was something cosmetic about Gordon. But Ken. Oh, just fancy going to bed with Ken.

Fanny began to walk again, her inner vision filled with Ken. She could see him so clearly, his weary smile, the lift of his chin as he looked up from the piano, the way his dark hair curled behind his ears. There was an easy rhythm about every-thing Ken did, an amused, tolerant enjoyment of life's basic idiocy that was immensely endearing. And yet, underlying that, there was a darker side. After the last Theatre Centre production, a girl who worked on the local paper had wanted to do a feature on Ken. 'Your life and loves, ambitions and disappointments – you know the sort of thing.' She had sug-gested this over a cup of coffee in the green room, smiling roguishly at Ken, who had responded with a gentle turning aside of the request. 'Dull reading, dear. Boringly conventional, I am.' But she had pursued him until he had suddenly banged down his coffee mug, cornered. 'Just give it a rest, will you?' he had said. And he had walked out without a word or a wave, leaving them all in an embarrassed silence while the reporter looked knowing and said she wasn't surprised.

Fanny turned down a side street, avoiding the necessity of passing her own house. She was going to the Theatre Centre. The decision seemed to have arrived without conscious debate and surprised her a little. She smiled. It was nice to be sur-prised.

The Theatre Centre looked shabbier by daylight, the paint on its windows dry and cracked. The front door, hardboard covered by Bunny Jackson in a moment of generosity, was painted bright red. At night it looked rich and welcoming but the clear light of mid-day revealed the shortcomings of Bunny's technique. The door was streaky, transparent toffee-apple red in some places, pillar-box thick in others. It was also, as Fanny expected, firmly locked.

She pushed her way through the dusty shrubbery at the back of the house until she reached the window of what used to be the pantry, now converted into the Ladies' Toilet. Underneath a brick half-buried in the soft earth she found several woodlice and a long, very rusty screwdriver blade, used by Fanny on several previous occasions. The window was of the sash type, loosely fitting. Fanny pushed the screwdriver blade up between the two panes and slid the catch across. Then she replaced the screwdriver under the brick, picked up her bag of books and, sliding the window up, climbed in. She made a safe if inelegant landing on the lavatory seat and fastened the window behind her. She washed her rust-stained hands in the little basin and then went to the Green Room in search of food.

The kitchen was equipped with coffee, sugar and powdered milk. Fanny also found the remains of a tin of salted peanuts, which she ate, and half a packet of Garibaldi biscuits. She made herself a cup of coffee, stuffed the biscuits into her raincoat pocket and went into the auditorium, carefully backing through the baize doors so as not to spill her coffee. She switched on the house lights with her elbow, walked down the gangway and sat in the front row to eat her makeshift lunch, in the seat where Ken always sat to direct rehearsals.

Us Lot was, Fanny thought, the most interesting thing they had ever done. It was Ken's idea and Ken had finalised the script but they had worked it out as a series of improvisations and almost everyone had contributed something. It was, simply, the story of a group of friends who preferred each other's company to that of any outsiders, but the play was put together like a musical, everyone elaborating the theme in the way which best suited him or her. Two of the younger girls who did tap dancing had a routine called 'See You' and the boys had a slapstick act based on the back-slapping enthusiasm with which old school buddies are apt to greet each other and developing into a knockabout fight. 'Saturday Afternoon' was a doggerel poem spoken in chorus by a group of girls planning what to buy and where to go, and Bunny Jackson, who was mad about cycling, did a comic version of an old 'pop' called the 'Push Bike Song' while he cycled slowly round Mollie Wimberley, whose tiny voice didn't matter because she had long blonde hair and looked gorgeous.

Fanny finished her coffee. Dusting crumbs from her lap, she got up and went up the shallow steps at the side of the stage. She switched on the working light but, disliking its fierce overhead glare, climbed the iron ladder to the lighting gallery which was usually presided over by Lee Haynes. He guarded it fiercely and Fanny revelled in the unusual opportunity to play with the lights as she wished. She supplied herself with a brilliant array of assorted colours, switched out the offending working light and dimmed down the house lights, then descended to the stage and stood in the wings, thinking about her part.

Fanny played Squib, the group's natural leader, cheerful and irreverent and – being parentless – completely independent. Squib lived a precarious life, cared for in theory by a hated aunt but actually living a half-criminal life of pilfering and sleeping rough. Fanny stared out at the brilliantly-lit stage, trying to get into her character's skin. Squib had to supply an element of excitement and danger to the group, but she had also to be wiser than they were. As their friendship deteriorated into the mutual dependence of a gang, Squib was the only one to realise it and to know what she must do. Following 'Try This', a number about experimenting with forbidden delights, came the crisis of the play in the shape of little Kathy Stebbing, entering with a packet of stolen cigarettes. 'Quite tricky, this bit, Fan,' Ken had said. 'Squib's very sick about the way things are going and she knows what she's got to do but we can't have her being holier-than-thou about it. None of your Saint Joan bit. Think it over.'

So Fanny had thought it over, in all slack moments at school, and in the bath, and in the fading moments before she went to sleep at night. Thought and thought about how she could do it and wished for a chance to try out ways of expressing the complex character of Squib without other people there to witness her attempts or to influence the thing she was trying to finalise. Now, for the first time, she had a chance to try and work it out.

She walked out on to the stage as Squib, feeling the black emptiness of the auditorium on her left – and turned back. Squib would not walk that way. The shoulders felt too important. Fussy. It needed to be an almost expressionless walk. She tried it again, making the entry for the final scene, to tell them she was going away. To pick a quarrel with them and destroy the whole set-up so that when she had gone it could start afresh with the final ironic song, 'Just Good Friends'.

Fanny went through the scene, speaking both her own lines and everyone else's, to get the timing right. She had to convey to the audience how much it cost her to renounce her friends, and her final exit was made down the steps into the auditorium, where she made her way up the gangway and out of the baize doors at the back of the theatre. Thus it was only the audience who saw her stricken face. To her left-behind friends on the stage, she presented a resolute back, stiff with unforgiveness.

As she approached the end of the scene, Fanny saw a widening chink of light appear and then close again under the baize doors. Somebody had come in. Tramp? Burglar? Her mind raced as she went on speaking, knowing that somebody was listening to her words. For a moment she contemplated abandoning Squib's character and inquiring as Fanny Anthony who it was down there – but the play ran on in her mind and Squib seemed immune from harm from the intruder, whoever it was.

'Who wants friends, anyway?' Squib said rhetorically to the people behind her as she stared out over the dark audience. 'Not me.' She began to walk down the steps, controlled and desolate. 'I – don't want – anyone.' She was on the floor. And there was somebody sitting in the middle of the front row.

'Oh!' said Fanny with a feigned start. 'Who's that?'

A tall figure got to its feet. 'Me. Haynes the Sparks. Got the afternoon off and thought I'd come in and sort out those spotlights. Sorry if I scared you.'

'Lee! No, it's all right. I just couldn't think who it was for a moment.'

Lee vaulted on to the stage and extended a hand to help Fanny up beside him. 'How did you get in?' he asked.

'I – I found the window of the loo was unlatched. Lucky for me! And how did you get in, come to that?'

'I nipped round and borrowed Ken's key. Went round to his school. I wanted to see him, anyway, to tell him about Mary. Here – she teaches at your school, doesn't she?'

'Mary Ross? Yes. Why?'

'She blew herself up with a geyser this morning. She's got digs in the same house as me, you know. Gave me a hell of a fright, I can tell you – heard this bloody great bang and rushed downstairs and there she was, lying under a heap of rubble.'

'So that's who it was – my father went out to someone but I didn't know it was Mary. How awful – is she all right?'

'She's in hospital but they say she'll be OK. She's very concussed, of course – cuts and bruises and that sort of thing – but talk about lucky! You should see the bathroom!'

'Did you go to the hospital with her?'

'Yes, thought I'd better. Seemed a bit tough, shoving her off in the ambulance all by herself. But by the time I got away from there it was so late there wasn't much point in going in to work so I rang them and said I had a touch of the cringe. Then I went to see Ken.' Lee grinned reminiscently. 'Poor old Ken, he *was* in a tizz! He's nuts about that girl, you know.'

Fanny froze. 'Is he?'

'Yes, blast his eyes. I fancied her like mad ever since she came to live in my digs, then like a twit I brought her round to this place and introduced her to Ken – and that was it. Instant click. You can always tell. When it happens like that there's nothing you can do about it, just say ah well, the best of British luck, mate.'

'Yes,' said Fanny bleakly, 'I suppose so.' Oh, Ken, Ken.

Lee moved past her to the lighting gallery ladder. 'Some mucky sod's left a coffee cup down there,' he said over his shoulder. 'And a biscuit packet. Bang in the middle of the front row.'

'It was me.'

'Oh. Well, you're the leading lady, I suppose you can leave your coffee cups where you like. You're doing rather well with that part, by the way – not that I know much about acting, of course.'

'Do you think so?'

'Wouldn't have said otherwise, would I? Is there any more coffee in the kitchen?'

'Heaps.'

'Make us a cup, there's a dear. If you've finished mucking about with my lights, that is.'

'All right,' said Fanny. She went down to the auditorium and picked up the biscuit packet and the dirty cup. Lee could have his old lights. The way she felt now, he could have the whole beastly place.

True to his word, Colin went in his lunch hour to see if Bobbie was still with the Brethren. Unlike Fanny, he tapped politely at the door and waited for an answer. None came, but the idle, mocking notes of the trumpet drifted infuriatingly from an upstairs window.

'Why can't he stop playing that thing and answer the blasted door!' Colin exclaimed aloud to a man in a jean jacket who was lounging against the wall nearby.

'Why's that?' asked the man. Something in his voice made Colin look at him again.

'Don't I know you?' he asked, frowning.

The man shrugged. 'I couldn't say.'

Colin stared at him trying to place the jean jacket and the slightly-too-old face.

'You looking for somebody, are you?' the man inquired casually – but there was an underlying note of genuine interest in his voice and in that moment Colin knew who he was.

'You're that copper!'

'Copper?'

'Down the unmade road by the school the other night. I was putting a frog in the hedge and you asked a whole lot of questions.'

'Really?'

'Oh, come off it,' said Colin savagely, 'there's no need to pretend it never happened. If I can talk about it, surely you can?'

The man glanced from side to side uneasily. 'You don't have to shout,' he said. 'It's a job, same as any other job.'

'It's not the same,' objected Colin. 'It gives you rights that ordinary people don't have. You ask questions and measure up the answers as if you were God or something.'

'That's going a bit far.'

'No, it's true! You've got a clear idea of how people ought

to behave, haven't you? You think you know what's right and what's wrong.'

'That's not our job. We just know what's against the law, that's all.'

'But the man on the beat decides whether to notice a thing or not. He can turn a blind eye if he wants to.'

'We use our discretion.'

'Discretion!' A dozen potential retorts, all equally crushing, leapt into Colin's mind. He thrust them away. This was no time for a wrangle with a stupid policeman.

'Look,' he said, man-to-man, 'I think my girlfriend's in there. Can you help me get her out?'

'What's her name?'

'Bobbie Rippon. Roberta, really—'

'Oh, she's safely back home. One of her school mates turned up this morning and walked in bold as brass, brought her out with no bother at all We drove them home.'

'Was that Fanny Anthony?'

'Now, that I couldn't tell you. I wasn't the interviewing officer.'

'Oh. But how did she get in?'

'Just pushed the door open.' The man smiled at Colin's puzzled face. 'That door isn't locked, you know. It just feels as though it is.'

Colin's shoulders sagged. He felt outwitted at every turn. 'I think I'll go round to her house,' he said, adding with sarcasm, 'if that's allowed, of course.'

'It's all right by me,' said the man mildly.

'What are *you* going to do?' asked Colin.

'Just stick around for a bit.'

'But why? If you've no quarrel with them ... ?'

The man narrowed his eyes fractionally. 'Listening to the music, aren't I?' he said. And Colin turned and walked away.

'Are you sure you'll be all right?' Marjorie asked her mother. 'I could ring Mrs Elkin and tell her to hang on until this evening, you know. It won't do Keron any harm to be left for a few hours.'

'You go, dear,' said Sylvia. Her face was white and crumpled, her eyes tiny between their puffy lids, but she was composed, her chin lifted in her usual autocratic style. 'Bobbie and I will be fine. Won't we, darling?'

Bobbie nodded. She felt dazed but relaxed, infinitely comforted by her mother's warm closeness. The events of the last twenty-four hours seemed as remote as a bad dream and the present reality was reassuring, although painfully sad. The house was subtly changed by her father's death and yet its deep familiarity made her feel that this was where she belonged. Her mother was, after all, the person closest to her. They needed each other. They loved each other. Bobbie slipped her hand into Sylvia's and squeezed it gently, sitting beside her on the settee by the fire. Sylvia's answering pressure was interrupted by Gordon's entry, which commanded her full attention.

'Gordon, dear – you've been so kind.'

'Rubbish. Old Cummings is the one to thank. Not many bosses would be so decent about time off. I'd better put my face in this afternoon, though, just to show willing.'

'Of course.'

Marjorie came across to kiss her mother. 'I'll ring you this evening, Mum, and we'll come over tomorrow and stay for a bit, won't we, Gordon? Keron's cot goes quite easily on top of the car – well, goodness, you know that!' Marjorie's laugh was oddly nervous. Gordon took her arm and said, 'Come on, love.'

'But are you sure. . . .'

'Come on.'

They all went to the front door where goodbyes were said and embraces made. Marjorie suddenly burst into tears and made a rush for the privacy of the car and Gordon said, 'She's a bit tired, I think.' He looked very worried.

'Gordon,' said Sylvia, 'don't come tomorrow. It's very sweet of you both to offer but I think Marjorie's had quite enough to cope with and little Keron might be upset.'

Gordon nodded, not without relief. 'Kids do sense atmospheres, I think. Anyway, we'll see. I'd better go.' He indicated the car and his weeping wife with a sideways jerk of his head and Sylvia nodded gravely.

'Of course. Thank you again, Gordon dear.'

Standing beside her mother on the doorstep, Bobbie watched the car depart.

'I suppose I shall have to learn to drive,' said Sylvia. Fresh tears brimmed in her eyes. Bobbie put her arm round her mother's shoulders as they turned to go in. 'You'll be a marvellous driver,' she said gently. 'You can do *anything* if you want to.'

'Can I?'

'Of course you can.'

'Oh, darling, you are sweet. And I've been so beastly to you but it was only because I worried about you so much. I don't want Gordon and Marjorie here, it's only you I want.'

'I'll always be here,' said Bobbie. Then, as she turned back to shut the door, she saw Colin approaching the house at a head-long run.

'Bobbie! Wait!' He slowed to a more dignified pace as he came up the path but when he reached the doorstep he was still out of breath. 'Bobbie!' He gripped her by both arms. 'Are you all right?'

'Yes, I'm fine.'

'I went round to that place and they said you'd come home, at least the policeman did, but I was so *worried* about you.'

Sylvia, unnoticed in her black dress, came forward from the shadowy hall to stand beside her daughter and Colin released Bobbie's arms a little guiltily.

'Bobbie, who *is* this?' inquired Sylvia with some hostility.

'It's Colin McIver – he carried my books home for me the other day, don't you remember?'

'No, I don't.'

Colin was still struggling to get his breath under control. 'I'm sorry to come rushing up like this, Mrs Rippon – I saw the car pull away and – I just wanted to catch Bobbie before she went in. I heard about the accident. I'm terribly sorry. It must be an awful shock.'

Sylvia closed her eyes. 'I suppose *everybody* knows.'

'If there's anything I can do,' Colin blundered on, 'anything at all — I'd be awfully willing.'

'Thank you,' said Sylvia icily. 'Bobbie, I think I will go and sit down.'

Colin watched her depart. 'I'm afraid I've upset her,' he said wretchedly, 'but I *had* to see you, Bobbie. Why on earth did you go off like that? Couldn't you have told me or something?'

'No, I couldn't. Things happened so quickly and — well, I just didn't think of it really.'

'I see.'

There was a long pause, then Bobbie said awkwardly, 'Look, I'll have to go in.'

'Yes.'

'It was nice of you to come.'

'Not at all.' Colin was deeply hurt. It was clear that his anxiety and his protective love counted for nothing. He had half-expected Bobbie to throw herself into his arms or to weep on his shoulder — at the very least, she should have looked pleased to see him. Instead, she stood silent on the doorstep, regarding him with no expression in those dark eyes which seemed so huge in her small face. 'I'd better be off, then,' he said. She nodded.

Colin turned and walked halfway down the garden path, then looked back. Bobbie was still standing in the doorway, watching him, but this time he thought she was crying. She made no move, but Colin saw that his suspicion was true. Tears were trickling down her face and she stood as if exhausted, too tired to wipe them away.

'Bobbie!' All resentment forgotten, Colin bounded back and enfolded Bobbie in his arms. 'Oh, darling, don't cry! Please don't!'

'I'm sorry,' whispered Bobbie. 'It'll stop soon.'

'There. It's all right. It's all right.'

In a little while Bobbie raised her head from Colin's shoulder and groped for a handkerchief. Colin gave her his and she blew her nose, then gave him the flicker of a smile. 'It's awful, this crying,' she said. 'It goes on and on.' Her lips quivered but this time she managed to fight back the tears.

'I think you're being very brave,' said Colin. 'You've had a terrible shock – you're bound to have a reaction. It's only natural.'

'I suppose so.'

'I do wish there was something I could do. Here – you've got a date with me tomorrow night. Had you forgotten?'

'Tomorrow? Friday?' Bobbie had lost count of the days.

'That's right. Tomorrow is Friday. I'll come round and see you but if you don't feel like going out you don't have to. We'll just do whatever you like. Bobbie. . . .'

'What?'

'I'm – I'm very fond of you. You know that, don't you?'

Bobbie nodded her head violently, smiling through an incipient onrush of fresh tears. A movement behind her caught Colin's eye and he became aware that Sylvia was standing in the hall.

'I think,' she said clearly, 'that your friend should either come in or go, Bobbie.'

Bobbie looked at Colin in something like dread.

'I'll go,' he said. 'See you tomorrow, Bobbie – don't forget!'

'I won't,' said Bobbie. Then she went in to her mother and shut the door.

'I brought you some grapes.'

'Oh, Ken!' Mary laughed. 'What a conventional thing to do!'

'I'm very well hospital-trained. Grapes the first day, maga-zines the second, choccies the third. No sitting on the bed, leave when the bell rings and don't wake the baby.'

'What baby?'

'Oh, there was always a baby. You're the first girl I've ever known who got herself into hospital because of a geyser instead of a baby. So beware.' Ken bent forward and kissed Mary lightly. 'How are you, anyway?'

'Oh, much better. I've stopped seeing two of everything but I've still got an awful headache. Having a baby would be much nicer, I think.'

'Don't speak of it, my lovely. Think of the loss to teaching it would be – you submerged in a tide of Ostermilk and me taken away gently raving in a straitjacket.'

'Ghastly. Have a grape.'

'Thank you. When are you getting out of this place? The sight of you lying there all pink and beautiful is getting me into such a state that I shall attack the ward maid on the way out.'

'You haven't seen her. She's got no teeth and she looks like a stick insect.'

'That's no good, then. I'll have to wait for you.'

'I can come out tomorrow, they think. Back to Mrs Mallalieu's lumpy bed.'

Ken ate grapes thoughtfully for a while. Then he said defensively, 'You wouldn't think of moving in with me, would you? Not in my present flat – I share it with two squash-playing bank clerks. But somewhere. No, of course not.'

'I would – think of it,' said Mary slowly, trying to conceal her delight, 'if you're sure. You've only known me for – what? Two days?'

'Solomon Olliphant Grundy,' said Ken. 'You know the rhyme—

> ' "Olliphant Grundy,
> Saw her on Monday,
> Took her out Tuesday,
> Bedded her on Wednesday,
> Moved her in on Thursday,
> Never got up Friday,
> Saturday or Sunday—
> Oh, what an end for
> Olliphant Grundy!" '

'You've been rehearsing that,' Mary accused him.

'Yes,' admitted Ken. 'I have. You haunt my thoughts, you see. Live with me, Mary, and be my love? If we start looking for a flat now, it'll be so long before we find one, you'll have plenty of time to go off me and escape.'

'I shan't go off you.'

Ken drew his finger gently down Mary's bare arm and laughed to see gooseflesh blossom on her skin. 'Mad girl,' he said. 'Be careful. No guarantees with Olliphant Ltd. It's a lousy firm.'

'Guarantees are never worth much,' said Mary. 'Everyone knows that.'

Ken smiled, a little sadly. 'I suppose they do,' he said.

'Mum, are you hungry?'

Sylvia exhaled a cloud of smoke and shook her head, not shifting her gaze from the television screen.

'Would you like a cup of coffee or something?' Bobbie persisted.

'No, thank you.'

'Can I get you a drink?'

'No, you can't!' snapped Sylvia. 'I do wish everyone would stop treating me as if I'm an old soak.' She resumed her truculent scrutiny of *Opportunity Knocks*, a programme which always moved her to passionate abuse of the talentless opportunity-seekers, but which she never missed.

'I thought I might open a tin of soup of something,' Bobbie ventured.

Sylvia turned her head slowly to look at her daughter with contempt. 'How you can think of *food*,' she said, 'at a time like this amazes me. But I suppose the young are essentially selfish.'

'It's not that I really *want* food,' said Bobbie. 'It makes me feel a bit sick to think about eating anything, but I'm so terribly empty.'

'Empty,' Sylvia repeated, giving the word a deeper significance. She turned her face back to the television screen and, staring at the spectacle of twin girls with spotted bows in their hair doing a tap-dance routine, gave a bitter laugh. 'What *do* they think they're doing? I could dance better than that when I was five. And just look at their legs. Like tree trunks.'

'Ghastly,' agreed Bobbie placatingly, and escaped to the kitchen. It was a pity Colin had come. Sylvia had resented his arrival furiously and there had been an angry outburst as soon as he had departed. 'You can't wait to bring another man into the house, can you? Never mind my feelings.' And so on. Bobbie had apologised, hugged her mother and promised that Colin meant nothing at all to her, agreed that he was a mannerless, blundering fool – and so peace, of a kind, had been restored.

But the brief period of warm companionship with her mother was gone, and Bobbie felt bereft. Since Colin's visit she had been flattering and placating and comforting towards her mother but Sylvia had remained distant though polite.

There was no tinned soup. Bobbie found some grated cheese left over from the omelettes Marjorie had made at lunch time and ate it on a slightly chewy piece of Ryvita. She drank some milk, then went back to the sitting room. Sylvia did not look up as she came in and Bobbie hovered irresolutely by the door.

'I think I'll go to bed,' she said. 'Will you be all right?'

There was no answer. After an awkward pause Bobbie said, 'Well – goodnight, then.'

'Goodnight,' said Sylvia. Bobbie abandoned her intention of kissing her mother and left the room quietly, closing the door carefully behind her.

Sylvia sighed and stretched out her feet. That child was a strain. So anxious to please. So lacking in flair. So *dull*. She got up and poured herself a gin and sweet Martini, and put a cherry in it.

The house was empty when Fanny came home from the Theatre Centre. She went upstairs and flung herself down on her bed, angry and miserable.

Bloody, bloody fool, she told herself, to imagine that Ken would think twice about some snotty little schoolgirl. Stupid to think that he even knew how she felt. If he *had* known, how would he have reacted? With amusement? Embarrassment? Disgust? Oh, please, not disgust. That was too painful a thought to be borne.

Fanny struggled hard to overcome the sense of hurt and loss which possessed her, trying to beat it into insensibility by ridiculing it. How absurd to feel let down by someone who had no idea that he was holding you up! But who else could be so warm and so funny and so sad? Wordlessly, Fanny spoke to Ken with the intimacy she would never know in reality. I shall never get over you, my love, she told him. No matter what other men I shall know, no matter if I even marry someone else and bear his children, I shall not forget you, my first and true love.

From downstairs, she heard the noise of the twins coming home. She smelt bacon being cooked, noted the sharp reek of burning toast ('Matthew! I put *you* in charge of the toast!') and heard the television set switched on at high volume. A little later Helen's car came in. Her key scratched in the lock and the television's volume was reduced. Onions were fried, followed by the spicy whiff of paprika and marjoram. Goulash for supper, then. Fanny lay inert on her bed. She toyed with the idea of ringing up Bobbie but decided against it, remembering her last glimpse of Bobbie and her mother clasped in each other's arms. She very much doubted whether Mrs Rippon's mother-love mood would last very long but she'd keep out of the way for the time being and let Bobbie make the most of it, if that's what she wanted.

Fanny turned her head to look out of the window. It was dark now but she could still see the pattern on the curtains and the bright indigo square which was the sky. Soon she would have to go downstairs. She felt profoundly disinclined to move.

To Fanny's irritation, the evening meal was a talkative one. She had intended to preserve a masterful silence about her activities of the afternoon but Helen's speculations about Bobbie's welfare forced Fanny to confess her intervention.

'I suppose somebody had to do something,' Helen said at the end of Fanny's story, 'but I'm really not sure that it had to be you. What's the school going to say?'

'What can they say?' returned Fanny without much interest. 'They can put me in detention – but they'll have to wait until next week because I owe Miss Perkins a detention I was supposed to go to tonight, so she's first in the queue.'

'I think you're being very silly. After all....'

'Oh, everyone's silly sometimes,' Stewart interrupted smoothly. 'Look at that girl I went to see this morning. She managed to blow up a geyser. Now, there's a daft thing to do if you like, and she's quite a bright girl, too. You'll know her I think, Fanny – someone said she teaches at your school.'

'Miss Ross. Yes.'

Dominic scented an unusual reticence in Fanny's response and said, 'Don't you like her?'

'Mind your own business,' said Fanny.

'Now, Fanny, he asked quite a reasonable question,' Helen protested – and Dominic, enjoying his mother's support, added, 'I bet she tells you off for wearing make-up.'

'You're just a snivelling little worm and you know nothing about it, so shut up,' said Fanny. She got up from the table. 'I'm going to the Theatre Centre.'

'Would you like a lift?' offered Helen.

'No, thanks.' Helen's car, as Fanny knew from past experience, provided a setting of unrivalled intimacy for 'straight talks'. And there had been quite enough talking for one night.

It was a dreadful rehearsal. To start with, Ken arrived nearly three-quarters of an hour late, and the cast were bored and annoyed. Some of them had lost patience and gone home.

'Deepest apologies,' said Ken. 'I've been to see our lovely Mary Ross, who came off second best in an argument with a gas geyser. I took her some grapes on behalf of us all – I knew you wouldn't mind. After all, the poor girl escaped death by a whisker.'

'Sounds as if she cut herself shaving,' said Fanny sourly. There was a general giggle but Ken glanced at her uneasily before he smiled. It was not like Fanny to be bitchy.

Rehearsal began but there was a sense of irritability which resulted in missed cues and forgotten lines. Fanny attacked her part with controlled ferocity, trying to sting the others into overcoming their half-heartedness.

'Fan,' said Ken at last, 'you're giving it the Medea treatment tonight. You look as if you're just about to murder your children. Can you brighten it up a bit?'

'I'm sorry,' said Fanny in a choked voice.

'It's like learning to drive,' Ken went on. 'It all goes great guns at first and then you strike a sticky patch where you don't know your garters from a gear stick. Don't worry about it – just relax a bit and it'll come back. You're probably a bit tired.'

'I am *not tired*!'

'Then you are overwrought, my darling,' said Ken easily, ignoring the mounting hysteria in Fanny's voice. 'Let's all break for coffee and tranquillisers. I'll go and put the kettle on with my own lily-white hands. *There* now.'

Ken got up from his seat in the front row and put his hand up to Fanny who was standing wretchedly on the stage. 'Come along, my lovely,' he said. 'Nobody rattles the cups quite like you do. Come and organise me.'

Fanny took his outstretched hand and jumped down from the stage, feeling a little sick with apprehension. Twenty-four hours ago this moment would have filled her with joy.

Ken filled the big kettle and put it on the gas ring. 'What's the trouble, Fan?' he asked, striking a match. 'Damn – I always burn my fingers. What's upsetting my leading lady?'

Fanny began to take cups out of the cupboard and arrange them on two trays on the counter top. 'Nothing.' Her voice, even to herself, sounded ludicrously strangled.

'Oh, come on. Tell your uncle Ken.'

Fanny stared down at the cups, angry and miserable and painfully aware that she had to make confession of her most secret and most beautiful dream. It had to be destroyed. Now.

'I – just don't think of you as an uncle,' she said.

The pause was agonisingly long. Then Ken put his finger under Fanny's chin and made her raise her head to look at him. 'Oh, Fanny,' he said gently, 'I don't deserve it.'

'No,' agreed Fanny, dealing roughly with her anguish, 'you don't. I just thought you did, that's all. I'm sorry. I didn't want to tell you.'

'Fanny, my lovely girl, don't be so hard-boiled. It's such a destruction. Listen.' Ken took both Fanny's hands in his. 'I tell you this truthfully. You are talented and beautiful and clear-thinking. You are my special joy and I care for you very much but. . . .'

'But you don't *love* me. You love Mary.' Even as she said it, Fanny regretted her words. It sounded a mean, impertinent statement, none of her business. 'I'm sorry,' she said. 'I shouldn't have said that.'

'Yes, you should. There's nothing people can't say to each

other. It's cowardice that shuts us up, not finer feelings. How did you know about Mary?'

'Lee told me. But he wasn't gossiping, honestly. It – it just wasn't like that.'

'Lee.' Ken frowned unhappily. 'Yes. Oh, Fanny, what can I say to you? It's going to sound so conventional. I'm not so far off fifty, married twice and mucked it up both times. You know all that. But you see, I'm like one of those fairground machines that don't give you your money back even if you win. Strictly for amusement only.' He smiled sadly at Fanny's troubled face. 'Now, being a thoroughly nice girl, I suppose you're worried about Mary, are you?'

'Well—'

'You needn't be. I'm pretty sure Mary will give me the push the minute I start to be a nuisance. She's a tougher egg than she looks, is our Miss Ross. I don't go round damaging people if I can help it.'

'People might want to be damaged,' Fanny ventured with a last flicker of hope.

'Once, perhaps. Twice, even. But nobody's mad enough to go on and on getting hurt. At least, I'm not.' Ken wilfully misunderstood her meaning.

'The kettle's boiling,' said Fanny. She watched Ken with tenderness as he turned off the gas and attempted to pick up the hot kettle with his bare hand. 'The kettle holder's on the nail,' she told him. She had not thought that it might be she who would damage Ken. She had always seen it the other way round.

'So it is,' said Ken. 'Oh, Lord, we haven't put the coffee in the cups.'

Fanny unscrewed the lid from the coffee jar. 'I'll spoon, you pour,' she said. 'Put the kettle back on the gas or it'll stop boiling.'

Ken did as she told him and then stood, pleating the blue felt kettle holder between his fingers, watching her spoon out the coffee. Fanny came round the side of the counter to reach the rest of the cups and he put his arm round her shoulders and hugged her to him. 'I'm sorry, Fanny,' he said gently. 'I really am.'

63

Fanny stifled the desire to burst into tears. 'It's all right,' she told him. 'You don't have to worry.' She finished the row of cups and added, 'You can fill these up now.'

Ken, obediently fetching the kettle, shook his head in admiration. 'Yes, ma'am,' he said.

Helen looked up from the driving glove she was mending.

'You're very late, Fanny.'

'I know. I went for a drink with some people from the Theatre Centre after rehearsal.'

'Where?'

'To the Three Tuns.'

'Well, I don't think you should. You're miles under age and—'

'I look eighteen.'

'That's not the point. And what about your school work? You've missed nearly all of today and you've done no homework – you'll get dreadfully behind.'

'It's all *right*, Helen, I'll do it at the weekend.'

'The point is, you need some time off,' put in Stewart. 'If you're working all weekend and every evening, you're bound to get over-tired.'

'I do wish people would stop telling me I'm tired,' said Fanny irritably. She dumped her bag on the floor and unbuttoned her coat, then went out to hang it up. When she came back Helen said, 'Why did you take your books with you? There's not much time to work at the Theatre Centre, is there?'

'I left them there this afternoon,' said Fanny.

'This afternoon? You went to the Centre this afternoon?'

'Yes, I just said so.'

'You mean, you didn't go back to school after you'd been to see Bobbie?'

'No, I didn't actually.'

'Oh, Fanny, *really*!'

'Look, why don't you just shut up!' Fanny blazed suddenly. 'I don't have to tell you where I'm going all the time and the more fuss you make the less likely I *am* to tell you – so just leave me alone!'

Helen squinted carefully at her leather glove, matching the

holes along the seam before she drove her needle through. 'You seem absurdly het up,' she observed. 'This Theatre Centre seems to have a very upsetting effect on your emotions. Are you having an affair with some boy there or something?'

'I wouldn't tell you about it if I was!'

'Obviously. That's why I have to ask, isn't it?'

'No, you don't have to. You're always so beastly cool and controlled, you just don't understand that people do things and feel things that *aren't* reasonable.'

'That's a bit unkind, Fanny,' said Stewart.

'Yes, I know it's unkind. But at least I do *know* it's unkind. I'm not unkind accidentally.'

'The trouble with you is, you're so obsessed with your own feelings, you think everyone who doesn't flatter you and pamper you is being unkind,' said Helen acidly.

'Oh, get stuffed. Begging your pardon, Stewart. I'm sure you do your best. I'm going to bed.' And Fanny left the room, banging the door behind her.

'You're a bit tough on her, Helen,' said Stewart.

'I know. But she's a tough girl. She'll walk over us with hob-nailed boots on if she's not made aware of her responsibilities. And I don't care what anyone says – she's having an affair with someone.'

'Oh, Lord.'

'You needn't worry. Judging by tonight's little outburst, it's probably over.'

'You women terrify me. You talk about logic and reason, yet when it comes to assessing how another person feels, it's all tea-cups and witchcraft.'

'Intuition,' said Helen with dignity, 'is merely the hypersensitive operation of the normal responses.'

'Bunkum,' said Stewart.

Bobbie woke sharply and stared wide-eyed at the slit of light under the door. There had been the sound of a crash downstairs, she was sure. She listened, straining her ears in the darkness until they hummed with silence. No. There was nothing. She turned over and closed her eyes.

Another sound came – an odd, rustling tinkle. Then the mutter of a voice. Bobbie jumped out of bed and put on her dressing gown. She went out on to the landing, where the light was on, and opened the door of her mother's room. A shaft of light fell across the tidy bed. Her mother was not there.

Bobbie started down the stairs and, turning on the half-landing, stopped to stare in horror down at the hall. It was littered with broken glass and in the middle of it Sylvia, on hands and knees, raked about petulantly with a cocktail stick.

'Mummy! What's happened?' Bobbie rushed down the rest of the stairs but stopped short of the hall floor, reluctant to venture over the broken glass in her bare feet.

'I's – tidying up,' Sylvia said thickly. 'Ol' bottles all empty and I's putting them in the dus' bin. Silly things slipp'ry. Bloody silly vinyl floor smash 'em all. An' I've los' my cherry.' She sat back on her heels and began to cry drunkenly. 'Oh, Bobbie, I've los' my little cherry. Glass broken, cherry gone, all I got's a silly little stick. Don't want stick.' She threw the cocktail stick away from her peevishly and ran her fingers through her hair in tipsy misery. As she did so Bobbie saw, to her dismay, that her mother's hands, gashed by the broken glass, were streaming with blood.

5 Friday

'Fanny!' Helen shouted up the stairs. 'Come on! You'll be awfully late!'

'Coming.' Fanny sounded calm.

Helen went back into the kitchen and pushed a few dishes into the washing-up machine.

'I like this muesli,' said Matthew. 'It's sort of munchy.'

'I put marmalade on mine,' said Dominic, 'but it makes the milk go funny.'

'It looks like sick,' said Matthew.

Helen frowned. 'Matthew, don't be so disgusting.'

'He's quite right, actually,' remarked Stewart, putting down the *Guardian*. 'That's what happens to milk when it gets into your stomach, you see, Matthew. It curdles.'

'I think we ought to have windows in our fronts like washing machines so you could see what's going on inside,' said Dominic.

'That book about babies had a picture of a woman with a glass front,' said Matthew. 'There was a vase of flowers beside her and I said that ought to be glass too, but Miss Billings said I was showing off.'

'So you were,' said Helen. 'I thought it was rather a nice book, actually. Sensitive.'

Fanny entered. 'What was?' She was wearing an ankle-length skirt of striped cotton and a long-sleeved blouse under a short-sleeved jersey top, the ensemble finished off by a long white cotton pinafore with frills on the shoulders.

'Fanny! What on earth are you dressed like that for? It's a school day.'

'I'm not going to school today,' said Fanny.

Dominic put his spoon down. 'If she's not going, neither am I.'

'Nor me,' said Matthew.

'Oh, yes, you are,' said Fanny calmly. 'But I am going round to see Bobbie and I'm sick of walking about in school uniform being stared at. When I've seen Bobbie I shall come back here and catch up with all my homework and make sure I'm word perfect in my part. There's a bit in the middle I'm not too sure of.'

'Oh, yes,' said Helen coldly, 'and what will you do after *that*?'

'I shall probably go to sleep,' said Fanny. 'Is there any coffee?'

Stewart laughed. 'Are you going to school on Monday?' he asked.

'Oh, yes,' said Fanny. 'It's art.'

'Stewart, you're not going to sit there and condone this behaviour, are you?' Helen was deeply scandalised.

'Yes,' said Stewart after a moment's thought. 'I don't think there's any alternative.'

'But we all have to *work*!' protested Helen.

'I've never agreed with you there,' said Stewart, 'but we won't argue that one this morning. Dominic, what are you doing?'

'Taking off my tie. If I'm not going to school then I don't need to wear it.'

'You *are* going to school!' said Helen with ferocity. 'Just because Fanny has gone mad it doesn't mean you two are going to loaf round the house all day. Finish your muesli.'

'I have.'

'Then go and pack your PE kit. It's Friday. You too, Matthew.'

Grumbling, the twins left the room.

Fanny sat down with her coffee. 'Can I have a look at the paper?'

'Hang on a minute,' said Stewart, immersed.

'You have got a cheek, Fanny,' Helen observed. 'You opt out of all your responsibilities and then try to pinch the perks of life as well.'

'Yes, of course,' said Fanny. 'You would, too, if you'd got any sense. Nobody's *asking* you to be all conscience-stricken.'

Stewart sighed and handed Fanny the paper. 'Here. Anything for a quiet life. Who'd be blessed with two articulate women first thing in the morning?' He glanced at his watch. 'I'd better get started. Got a few letters to write before morning surgery.'

He stood up, then added, 'There'd be no doctors in *your* world, Fanny.'

'Oh, I don't know,' said Fanny, glancing through the arts page, 'work for some people *is* self-indulgence.'

'I'll remember that,' said Stewart.

Helen arrived at the bookshop feeling ruffled. It was very annoying to leave one's daughter making toast in the kitchen when she ought to be at school. Helen was not in the habit of introspection but now, seeking to analyse exactly why it was that she felt so aggrieved, she found herself suffering from a deep sense of injustice. It seemed so unfair that, after years of irksome responsibility, she should be accused of a lack of selfishness.

She unlocked the door, picked up the letters which were lying on the mat and switched on the lights. Where was Colin? He should have been here by now. She glanced cursorily through the mail. Invoices, telephone bill, a brochure from a shop-fitting firm and an invitation to a symposium on Violence in Children's Fiction to be held in Venice next month. You should go, Fanny would say. You can afford it. Just pack a bag and go.

What would Venice be like in November? Thin sunshine slanting across the Piazza San Marco where the chairs and tables outside the cafés would be empty, their crosshatching of legs and backs as black as winter twigs. And there would be the occasional brandy-sipping Venetian, as plump as a pheasant, or an out-of-season tourist hung about with cameras. Oh, Italy.

'Sorry I'm late,' said Colin, scrubbing his feet vigorously on the mat.

'Oh. Yes, you are rather. Never mind, there haven't been any customers.'

Colin was a little disappointed by this leniency. It would have been easier to break his news to Helen in one of her masterful moments.

'I've no particular reason for being late,' he continued belligerently. 'I was just thinking and I didn't notice the time.'

'M'm.' Helen was frowning over a letter in her hand.

'You see, I can't really go *on* like this,' pursued Colin. 'Are you listening?' he added irritably.

'Yes,' said Helen. 'Like what?'

'Oh, the same old thing day after day. Just being a shop assistant. I mean, it's not going to get me anywhere.'

'You mean you're leaving.'

'Yes.'

'When?'

'I don't know. I've got to sort things out.'

'What are you going to do?'

'I thought I might hitch-hike to Israel and work on a kibbutz. Or work for IVS or something – I've got to do *something*. I must see a bit of the world and – well – just *live* a bit.'

'What about Bobbie?'

'*What* about Bobbie?'

'Have you told her?'

'No, not yet.'

'But, Colin, I thought you—'

'Hang on a minute. I'm not going back on what I said. I do care about Bobbie and I want to be with her, if she wants to be with me. But I can't shape my whole life round somebody else. I don't even know if she'll want me. I saw her yesterday and – well, maybe I'm being daft, but I think she cares more for her mother than she does for me. I just didn't seem to belong.'

'Of course you didn't belong! Just imagine if your father had died and some girlfriend of yours came bursting in – how would *your* mother like it?'

'She'd never be unwelcoming,' said Colin positively. 'Any friend of mine could come into our house at any time and share what we had – even if it was grief. But then, we're not your stiff-upper-lip people, are we? We don't *mind* people knowing how we feel.'

'Oh, for God's sake, Colin! The trouble with you is, you feel you haven't been taken enough notice of. All right, *go* and make the desert blossom if that's what you think you've got to do – but don't expect the rest of us to clasp our hands in admiration.'

'That's a beastly thing to say!' said Colin hotly. 'Why shouldn't I travel if I want to?'

Helen stared at him for a moment, then slammed the invitation card down on the counter. 'Then why shouldn't I?' she said. 'I am going to Venice next month and to hell with the lot of you. I'm preached at on all sides about being old-fashioned and inhibited, and nobody else thinks twice about "doing their own thing". Well, OK. I'm going to be irresponsible. If you're not here to run the shop then I'll close the blasted thing and if it never opens again then I just *don't care*.'

Colin laughed. 'Good for you!' he said. 'When are you going?'

Helen opened two or three invoices while her bravado ebbed away and then said sulkily, 'I probably shan't.'

'That's ridiculous!' said Colin. 'You're just making a martyr of yourself.'

'I am *not*! What on earth have I done to deserve all this abuse? Do you know what I think?'

'What?'

'I think that young people feel terribly guilty because of all they've been given. They know they've done nothing in their whole lives except *take* – take food, take money, take love, take time, take attention – and they suddenly become aware that they feel conscience-stricken about it. So what do they do? They try to remove this uncomfortable guilt by blaming their parents for causing it.'

'That's probably true,' said Colin after a thoughtful pause, 'but most parents make their kids feel so useless. I mean, how can parents and children get to know each other as adults when there's this terrible load of obligation between them? It's all to do with being well-off, of course. The children of peasant people earn their keep all along, because they work with their parents. *They* don't feel guilty.'

Helen sighed. 'No,' she said, 'I suppose they don't.'

She gathered up her letters, adding the Venice invitation, and stacked the handful neatly beside the *Writers' and Artists' Year Book*, to be dealt with later.

'When is your Venice thing?' asked Colin.

'Next month, thirteenth to the twentieth. But I shan't go.'

'Yes, you will. I'll look after the shop. I promise I won't leave before then.'

'Leave when you like.'

'Oh, come on!' he chided her.

Helen looked at him, eyebrows raised indifferently, and tried to meet his warm smile with hauteur. It was no good. Despite herself, she smiled back. She shook her head ruefully.

'Venice,' she said. 'Good Lord, I must be mad.'

'And about time, too,' said Colin.

Fanny waited a long time before Bobbie answered the door.

'Hello, love,' she said as it finally opened. 'I just came to see how you're feeling.'

'Fanny! You're not at school.'

'No. Came to see you.'

'I was going to go to school this morning, but I didn't wake up. Come in.' Bobbie was wearing a pink dressing gown. Her feet were bare and she looked crumpled. 'I'll make some coffee,' she said.

'I'll do that. You go back to bed. I'll bring some up.'

'No, I'll get dressed. I'll be down in a minute.'

Fanny went into the kitchen and was immediately reminded of Gordon's little onslaught the previous day. Although she did not much like Gordon as a person, it was very flattering to be thought attractive. She filled the electric kettle and plugged it in, then found mugs and sugar, instant coffee and spoons. Thanks to Marjorie, everything was clean and in its place. A milk-filmed glass and a knife that had been used for spreading butter stood on the draining board so Fanny washed them and tore off a length of kitchen roll to dry them. This done, she threw the crumpled paper into the kitchen bin – and stared. The open lid of the bin revealed that it was almost full of blood-soaked Kleenex. A glint of reflected light caught Fanny's eye and, poking cautiously, she found that the bin also contained a large quantity of broken glass. Fanny looked thoughtful as she poured boiling water into the coffee cups. Somebody had had a very nasty accident.

Bobbie came in, tugging a comb through her mop of frizzy hair. 'I feel an awful mess,' she said. Fanny looked at her friend's hands but could see only a small plaster round the end of one finger.

'Did you cut yourself?' she asked.

'No, it's just a hangnail that I bit off and it was a bit sore,' said Bobbie. 'I do wish I could stop biting my nails.'

'Who bled, then?' asked Fanny baldly. 'All that Kleenex in the bin.'

Bobbie blushed. 'Mum tripped over and broke a glass. She cut her hand.'

'It must have been some cut. When did that happen?'

'Last night. I like your blouse, Fanny. Where did you get it?'

Fanny ignored the question. 'Is your mother all right? What did you do?'

'I found an old pillow case and tore it up. There didn't seem to be any bandages and plasters wouldn't do.'

Fanny wondered whether to ask the unvoiced question which was hanging between them and decided that she would.

'Was she drunk?'

Bobbie looked stricken.

'I'm not being beastly,' said Fanny in a matter of fact voice. 'I just think you've been doing the brave little heroine bit quite long enough, that's all, and it's time you knew it isn't a secret and it isn't the end of the world if other people know about it.'

'How long have you known?'

'I've suspected for ages. You've almost told me several times – but it was Colin, really, who made it certain.'

'*Colin?*' Bobbie was shocked. 'You mean he went round saying—'

'He didn't go round saying anything. He just asked Sandie if she knew whether your mother drank a lot because he thought she was pretty pie-eyed when he took you home one night and he was worried about you. He really cares about you, you know, Bobbie.'

'Does he?'

'I'm sure he does. You can always tell.'

Bobbie smiled and took a sip of coffee. 'Anyone would think you had years of experience!'

'Well, I'm getting more experienced each day,' said Fanny. For an instant she felt tempted to tell Bobbie about Ken, but decided not to.

'What do you mean? What have you been up to?'

'Your brother-in-law kissed me passionately in this very kitchen yesterday.' Gordon was easy to talk about.

'Gordon? No!'

'Oh, yes.'

'But, Fanny, you shouldn't – I mean—'

'Oh, don't look so horrified – it was only a kiss. Marjorie looked a bit suspicious because of my red face but I think she put that down to the gin.'

'Fanny, you're just *awful*.'

'No, I'm not, I'm a tonic. Look at you – all het up about your problems until I come along and then you're so busy being shocked about me that you forget all about you.'

Bobbie shook her head and laughed. 'You're crazy.' She finished her coffee and when she looked up her face was grave again. 'Fanny, what shall I do about Mum?'

'I don't know. Perhaps there's nothing you can do. I'm not even sure what sort of a problem it is. I mean, the people at the Theatre Centre drink, and my parents drink, but when do people stop being just drinkers and start being alcoholics? What's different about your mum, if anything?'

'I don't know. Honestly, Fanny, she's a marvellous person in lots of ways. When Marjorie and I were small I used to think she was lovely. She was always a bit frightening but she was so beautiful, she was always exciting. She had a black evening dress she wore once when she went somewhere with Dad – it had those wispy floaty feathers all round the neck and she had long sparkly earrings. Oh – I don't know. I used to think she just got very tired. Sometimes she'd be asleep on the floor when I came in from school and I couldn't wake her up ... and then when she *did* wake up she looked awful and she'd say she had a terrible headache and go off to bed. And Dad used to be so angry and I never understood why. I think perhaps Marjorie knew but we never talked about it. I was so much younger, you see, she thought of me as her baby sister. And then things started to change. Dad wasn't here much, Marjorie got married and went away and Mum – seemed to be angry all the time. Not just fits of temper – she always had those – but she sort of smouldered all the time like a volcano. And then one day I suddenly fell in about her drinking.'

'How?'

'I'd lost my fountain pen. I'd hunted for it all over the place and I couldn't find it so I started looking in silly places, you know the way you do, inside the piano and under the beds. It was a sort of obsession. I couldn't stop thinking about it, as if something awful would happen if I didn't find it. I've always had this feeling that awful things were going to happen.'

'So?'

'Well, I'd looked absolutely everywhere I could think of. And then I remembered this cupboard we've got, above the downstairs lavatory. It's something to do with the way the levels go, the architect had a bit of space left under the stairs and he made it into this silly cupboard that we never used because you had to stand on a chair to get at it. We kept the yog nest in it.'

'The what?'

'The yog nest. We used to make natural yoghurt ages ago, and the pots had to be kept warm in a kind of polystyrene bowl that we called the yog nest, but we hadn't used it for ages because the culture died.'

'So you looked in the cupboard,' prompted Fanny.

'Yes.' Bobbie paused. 'It was full of empty bottles. Gin and sherry and something called VP wine. Heaps and heaps of them.'

'Good Lord. What did you do?'

'Nothing. I couldn't think at first how they'd got there. What it meant. And then I smelt that acidy sort of smell coming out of them and I suddenly knew. But I felt so awful about knowing that I just pretended I didn't. I shut the cupboard door very quietly and I never looked in it again.'

'Did you ever find your pen?'

'No.'

'And the bottles were the Awful Thing.'

'Yes.'

'Poor old Bob. What really happened last night, then? You may as well tell me now you've started.'

'This awful crash woke me up. So I came down the stairs and she'd dropped all these bottles and glasses. I don't know where she was going with them, but she was grovelling about in the broken glass—'

'Whatever for?'

'She said she'd lost her cherry.' Bobbie began to laugh but it turned into a sob.

'Let's have your coffee mug and I'll wash it. So you had to clear up all the broken glass and deal with cut hands?'

Bobbie nodded. 'Oh, Fanny, I do hope she's all right. Some of the cuts looked awfully deep and I didn't know if there was glass still in them. She kept crying and saying she was sorry and I couldn't get her to keep still.'

'Why didn't you ring your doctor?'

'I thought of it, but she doesn't like him and there'd have been an awful fuss.'

'Why doesn't she? Who is he?'

'Dr Robinson. I don't know why. She had some sort of argument years ago and she won't go and see him now.'

'But why didn't she change to someone else?'

'I don't know. She wouldn't ever talk about it. I looked at her this morning but she's still fast asleep.'

Fanny frowned thoughtfully. 'Bob, why don't you come and stay with us for a bit? You've had such a rotten time lately and I know Helen wouldn't mind. She's great about practical things.'

'I'd better not,' said Bobbie. 'I'd better be here when Mum wakes up. And anyway, Colin's coming round this evening.'

'That's nice,' said Fanny absently, still pursuing her half-formed plan. 'But come to lunch, anyway. I shouldn't think your mum will feel like much, will she?'

'No, she never eats until the evening at the best of times. But I'm not very hungry, Fanny.'

Fanny wiped the draining board briskly. 'I must be off,' she announced. 'I've got heaps to do, so I'll leave you to cope with your mum for a bit. I'll call for you on the way home for lunch. OK?'

'I don't know—'

'See you, then.' Giving Bobbie no time to argue, Fanny pointed a finger in the direction of the ceiling, indicating the still-sleeping Sylvia. 'Best of luck!' she said – and left.

As Miss Beacon entered the room, 4N struggled half-heartedly to its collective feet.

'Sit down, girls. Mrs Newley, I wonder if I may have a word with these people for a minute?'

Mrs Newley, prewarned, smiled her assent.

Miss Beacon thrust her hands into her jacket pockets in a stance which thirty years of teaching had made automatic.

'I have come to tell you the very sad news that Roberta Rippon's father died yesterday.' Miss Beacon observed from the lack of surprise which her announcement caused that the girls were already aware of this fact. 'I think it is much better for you all to know this rather than have the news spreading by hearsay,' she continued, unperturbed. 'Roberta will not be returning to school for a few days but when she does, she will need your kindness and understanding. Don't be too obviously sympathetic – just be your natural selves but exercise a little extra consideration. Now, does anyone want to say anything?'

'Is Fanny staying at home to be with Bobbie?' asked Mary Coppard. Miss Beacon was not aware of Fanny's continued absence but, after only a second's pause, she said smoothly, 'Understanding companionship is of the greatest possible value, I think.' The girls nodded approval. Then Sandie McIver put up her hand.

'Yes, Sandie?'

'I'm not saying this to be cheeky,' began Sandie carefully, 'but – could I ask if you'll say the same thing to the staff, Miss Beacon?'

'I see no necessity to do so.'

'But if you're feeling miserable,' Sandie persisted, 'and someone gives you a heck of a telling-off, then it's just about the last straw, you know?' Her voice was more markedly Scottish in her anxiety.

'I am sure you need have no worries on that score,' said Miss Beacon firmly. The girls eyed her without conviction although most of them looked respectful. Miss Beacon sighed inwardly. 'Now, don't all look so serious,' she said brightly. 'That's no way to cheer up your friend, is it?' Nobody smiled.

'Thank you, Mrs Newley,' said Miss Beacon. 'That's all I have to say.' She left the room. The fourth year was always awkward. Next year, when O-level pressure began to make itself felt, there would be a marked improvement in these girls' attitude. There always was.

'But don't you *see*, Helen, Bobbie would be much better with us, just for a bit, anyway.'

While Fanny argued with her mother, Colin tried to efface himself in the Reading Corner, busily rearranging the little chairs. He was not included in the conversation but it was impossible not to overhear it.

'I'm sorry, Fanny.' Helen was pink-faced and defensive. 'It's not that I'm unsympathetic, but it simply isn't up to me. Surely you can see that? Bobbie's mother must be terribly upset and she won't want to be left alone at a time like this.'

'All Bobbie's mother wants is a bottle of gin,' said Fanny. 'Doesn't she, Colin? You said she was an alcoholic just the other day, didn't you?'

Colin flinched under Fanny's sudden attack. 'Oh, that was just a superficial impression,' he said hastily, glared at by Helen. 'I mean, I'm not an expert.'

'Coward,' said Fanny.

'No, Fanny, he's just being rational,' protested Helen. 'You do have this tendency to be over-simple in your judgements. Black and white, for me or against me.'

'But it's nothing to do with *me*!' cried Fanny. 'It's – oh, what's the sense?' She rushed to the door, opened it and turned to say, 'Just *sit* on the fence. And I hope the pair of you split right up the middle!'

'Vulgarity will get you nowhere,' Helen called after her – but Fanny had gone.

She stormed up the High Street, swept along by her mental tirade of abuse for all the narrow-minded, mealy-mouthed forces of convention which made the world unnatural and mean, past the shop windows full of Crimplene jerseys and tinned rice pudding and awful shoes.

'Watch it!' A man in a white coat carrying a large television set staggered past her as she halted for him. 'Ta!' He dumped the set in his van. 'We do seem to meet in odd places, don't we?'

'Lee!'

'You in a hurry? Drop you somewhere if you like.' He indicated his van.

'I don't really know where I'm going,' confessed Fanny. 'Just sort of generally *away*.'

'Like that, is it?' Lee grinned. 'I know how you feel. Here, hang on a minute while I fetch one more portable.' He darted back into the shop. Fanny thought rapidly. She was determined that Bobbie should at least come to lunch but it was too early to collect her yet. And Fanny felt very disinclined to go home. As Lee came out of the shop with a small portable set, Fanny yielded to a sudden impulse.

'Actually,' she said, 'I thought I'd go and see Miss Ross. Er – Mary. Is she still in hospital?'

'Last I heard, she was coming out this morning,' said Lee. 'Ken was going to fetch her home in that little banger of his. I told him, I said, that's enough to give you concussion. Tell you what, I'm going up my way, so we'll drop in at Farringdon Hill and see if she's back. You can ask Mrs Mal and if she isn't, I'll run you down to the hospital. OK?'

'That's great,' said Fanny. 'Are you sure it isn't a nuisance, though? I could easily walk.'

'The chance to have a smashing bird in my van is never a nuisance,' said Lee. 'So get in and don't be daft.'

Fanny got in, wondering what had impelled her to go and see Mary. Perhaps anything was better than nothing, no matter how painful. They drove along for a while in silence, then Lee said reflectively, 'Yes, poor old Ken really has got it bad for that girl.'

Shut up, thought Fanny savagely. Keep your bloody observations to yourself, you clumsy, blundering fool. Aloud, she said casually, 'Has he?' The pause was a little too long, the tone a fraction too innocent. Lee grinned and said, 'Thought so.'

'Thought what?' asked Fanny crossly.

'You were a bit gone on Ken yourself, weren't you?'

Fanny stared out of the van's side window. Maddeningly, the street was suddenly blurred by tears. It was *beastly* of him to come out with it like that.

'Hey,' said Lee. 'I'm sorry. I didn't realise it was that bad or I wouldn't have mentioned it. Forgive me?' He put his left hand over hers and squeezed it. After a moment, Fanny squeezed back. You couldn't really be cross with Lee.

'Tell you the truth,' he said, 'I nearly asked you yesterday if you'd like to come out with me some time. But you shot off so quick I never got round to it.'

'I don't know,' said Fanny weakly.

'It's all right if you don't want to. No skin off my nose. I just thought, there's me all cut up about Mary and you moping over Ken, so why don't we get together for an hour or two? I'm not asking you to be my girlfriend or anything – just come and have a drink and we'll cry on each other's shoulders.'

'I think that would be super,' said Fanny. 'I wasn't being snooty or anything, honestly – I just couldn't think for a moment. I didn't know anyone knew about Ken. Makes you feel a bit of an idiot.'

'Who isn't?' said Lee.

They arrived at the tall house on Farringdon Hill and Lee stopped the van. 'Here we are,' he said, 'and no sign of That Man's car, so you won't run into him on the stairs. Nip out and ask Mrs Mal if Mary's back and give me a wave if she is. I'll wait.'

'That's lovely,' said Fanny. 'Thanks.' She prepared to get out but Lee detained her with a hand on her arm.

'You coming to rehearsal tonight?'

'Yes.'

'We'll go and have a drink afterwards, then. OK?'

Fanny laughed. 'That'll be two nights running. Lots of us went round to the Three Tuns last night with Ken.'

'Not me, though. Thursday is my evening class night. I'm doing an audio course. And we won't go to the Three Tuns.

We'll go and be miserable all by ourselves at the Queen's Head.'

'Yes, we will.'

'And you won't scream for help if I kiss you goodnight?'

'No.'

'Great.' And suddenly Fanny found herself being kissed, not goodnight, she thought rather wildly, not in a television service van in the middle of the morning. Determined not to seem astonished, she slid her arm round Lee's neck and felt how hard his shoulders were under the white cotton of his overall. He smelt faintly of machine oil and tobacco and Fanny decided that she liked it.

Lee was too close to Fanny to see her face as a whole but he scanned it at close quarters feature by feature until he came to her mouth and then he kissed her again.

'Steady,' he said to himself aloud. 'Don't go berserk, Haynes. If we stay here much longer the shop will send out a search party.'

'A posse of angry customers,' said Fanny.

'All screaming about their wonky line-holds.'

Fanny laughed and opened the van door. 'What did you say your landlady's name was? Mrs Mal?'

'Mrs Mallalieu, properly speaking, but what a name! And what a woman!' Lee rolled his eyes.

Fanny looked at him doubtfully. Was this Mrs Mallalieu another of Lee's conquests?

'Go on,' said Lee. 'She won't eat you.'

Fanny climbed the steps to the ornate front door and rang the only bell which did not have a name beside it. None of the others said Mallalieu. After a long pause, the door was opened by an immensely fat woman who said, on the tail of a wheezy cough, 'Yes?'

'Is Miss Ross at home?'

'She's ill.'

'I know. That's why I've come. But is she here?'

Without giving a direct answer, Mrs Mallalieu moved aside from the door, leaning her head a little sideways to indicate that Fanny should enter. 'I hope this isn't going to be a habit,' she grumbled, 'people coming all hours of the night and day. I'm very busy, you know.' She retreated into the dark hall, leaving Fanny to wave reassuringly at Lee, who waved back and moved off in his van. Fanny shut the door.

'Upstairs,' wheezed Mrs Mallalieu. 'Two flights. I won't come up, if you don't mind.'

'Of course not,' said Fanny, relieved.

On the first landing a metallic rasping noise attracted her attention to the shattered bathroom. In it, a man in a very dirty boiler suit was cutting through a length of pipe with a hacksaw. 'Mornin'!' he said cheerfully, seeing Fanny. 'What d'you think of this lot, then?' He indicated the rubble-strewn bathroom, which was darkish because of the newspapers pinned across the empty window frames.

'Quite a mess!' said Fanny.

The man straightened up. 'If you ask me,' he said confidentially, 'whoever blew up this little lot did the old girl a favour. A real favour.'

'Goodness,' said Fanny politely, feeling a little like Alice in Wonderland.

'She said to me, Mr Dovedale, she says, what shall I do with my bathroom? Well' – the man gave a gap-toothed bark of laughter – 'I could 'ave told 'er. But whoever done this made a lovely job of it. A really lovely job.'

'I'm sure she's very pleased,' said Fanny. And she went on up the stairs. Fancy Miss Ross living here, she thought as she reached the narrow top landing. What a dreary place. Will I live in places like this? I suppose I will, if Miss Ross does. She tapped on what she hoped was Mary's door.

'Come in!'

After the dark landing the room was surprisingly bright. Mary was in bed, her head raised from the pillow to see who her visitor was.

'Fanny!' She sat up. 'Goodness, how nice of you to come!'

Fanny suddenly felt very empty-handed. She had come impetuously, out of a masochistic desire to confront her rival and she realised, with some shame, that she had hardly thought of Mary as a person. Now, sitting tousle-headed in bed in a long-sleeved white cotton nightie, Mary looked very real. And very pretty.

'I just thought I'd come and see how you are,' said Fanny. 'It was a sort of impulse. I mean, I'm not an official deputation or anything.'

Mary laughed and then stopped laughing quickly and shut her eyes for a moment.

'Does your head hurt?' asked Fanny.

'Just a bit if I make a noise or move it about,' said Mary. ' "Only when I larf", as they say.'

'I thought you'd be all bandaged up.'

'Oh, I was at first. I kept coming to and being sick and going off again. One time when I came to they were hitting my knees with a little hammer and I thought, this is mad, and then I'd gone again.'

'Reflexes.'

'That's it. I suppose you know all about that sort of thing, being a doctor's daughter. It was your father who came yesterday but I don't really remember much about him except that he seemed awfully kind. Will you thank him for me?'

'Yes,' said Fanny. Suddenly there was an awkward pause. The question of Fanny's absence from school loomed large.

'How are all the girls?' inquired Mary obliquely.

'Oh, fine. Everyone sends their love.' Fanny decided that she would have to make some explanation, since Mary was obviously determined to be tactful. 'I'm not away from school only because I came to see you – it's because of Bobbie.'

'Oh, Bobbie! Yes, what happened about her? Did she come back?' Mary flinched as her eagerness caused another twinge, but continued to look interested.

Fanny recited the whole story, but without mentioning Mrs Rippon, and Mary listened attentively. At the end of it she gave a sigh. 'Isn't it sad,' she said. 'There's this community we call a school supposed to be all *about* young people, and yet someone like Bobbie can feel completely alone in it. You'd think we could at least provide someone she could talk to, wouldn't you?'

'I expect there was, really,' said Fanny, 'but talking to people isn't thought of as very important at school, is it? Not unless they've done something wrong and then they get a talking-to. And that's different.'

'Quite different,' Mary agreed. 'It's all so *formal.* It's much better than it used to be, I suppose, but. . . .'

'It's not real,' interrupted Fanny.

Mary stared at her, puzzled. 'Not real?'

'It's all a sort of fantasy. I know it's *about* real things – I mean, maths is essentially true and geography tells you where the world's minerals are and all that sort of thing, but you don't sort of *know* it's true. It all comes out of a book the same as a story does but one is fact and the other is fiction and yet the fiction can seem much more convincing than the fact. Do you know what I mean?'

'Oh, yes I do,' said Mary. 'I never thought of French as anything more than tables of verbs until I went to France and didn't know what the word for "toothbrush" was.'

'It's an act of faith,' Fanny went on. 'They tell you it's true and the book says it's true but believing what they say is like giving yourself to someone else's mind. You have to just shut your eyes and believe it. But I don't really think I believe in anything except what I can see and hear and touch. That's what I mean about school – the real thing about it is sitting at a desk and knowing it's got a splintery bit on the side that you catch your tights on if you're not careful. And you'll be sitting at the same desk looking at the ink stains on the wood that you've looked at hundreds of times before and you know the shapes of them so well that you can see them in your sleep. That's what's real – and it's *so boring*!'

'Oh, Fanny, how awful. Do you feel like that all the time?'-

'Not absolutely all of it,' Fanny conceded. 'I can get lost in a book sometimes and just occasionally if a discussion gets going it can make you forget the time, but mostly it drags.'

'I know what you mean. I used to work in a café as a holiday job and it was quite interesting for the first day or two and after that the time just crawled past. I used to bet myself that I wouldn't look at the clock for ten minutes but when I looked there'd be only about four minutes gone. It must be like that for thousands of people every single day.'

'Ghastly,' said Fanny with feeling. 'No wonder they go on strike. I wonder if it's always been so boring? When you talk to old people, they seem to remember such interesting things.'

'It's the interesting things you *would* remember, of course,' said Mary, 'but there probably wasn't time to be bored then. Life must have been much harder with no machines or cars or telephones.'

'Yes, but they didn't have to sit down in one place for hours at a time.' Fanny was unrepentant. 'I think there's too much education. It's all fantasy. It separates people off from themselves – makes them escape in their minds.'

'But, Fanny, people *want* to escape!'

'Not into hours of Latin and maths, they don't,' said Fanny firmly. She thought for a minute. 'What I really mean is, I think everyone should do what they *want* to do. I don't see why they should be made to feel a failure if they don't get to university.' Mary started to say something but Fanny rushed on. 'Education's thought to be such a Good Thing, that parents set their hearts on their children being graduates and the schools tot up scholarships like Red Injuns counting scalps – the pressure is enormous. And besides, everyone talks about university as if it's terrific fun, so you feel you may be missing something.'

'It *is* fun,' said Mary. 'But then, I never wanted to do anything else. What about you – what do you want to do?'

'Me? Oh, I don't know. I'd really like to go on the stage, but that might be later. There's a whole world out there waiting to be got at, and I want to get at it! I want to travel and find myself in weird places and do things that are dangerous and peculiar. What I think would be absolute bliss would be to find a reality that's so extraordinary that you couldn't imagine anything stranger – a sort of fantasy come true.'

Mary laughed. 'It sounds terrifying,' she said. She sat up and attempted to rearrange her pillows and Fanny jumped up to help her.

'There's a cushion on this chair,' she said, 'shall I put it under the pillows to plump you up a bit? I'm sure you'd be more comfortable.'

'Thank you,' said Mary. 'That feels lovely.'

A silence fell between them.

'Is there anything you need?' Fanny asked. 'Can I get some fruit or anything?'

'No, thank you, I'll be fine. A friend of mine is coming this evening and he said he'd bring some bits and pieces. It's very sweet of you, though.' Mary's smile was open and happy and Fanny felt ashamed of her resentment. She glanced at her watch. Ten to twelve.

'I'd better go,' she said. 'I promised I'd be home for lunch.'

'Of course. Thank you so much for coming. It's been lovely talking to you.'

'I've enjoyed it, too,' said Fanny, realising with surprise that she spoke the truth. 'Will you be back at school on Monday?'

'Oh, I should think so,' said Mary confidently.

'Good. See you there, then.'

'Yes. Lovely. Bye-bye.'

'Bye.'

As Fanny let herself out she felt very confused. Mary was a teacher and yet Fanny had seldom talked to anybody with such freedom and understanding. In different circumstances, she felt sure that Mary and she would be close friends. But Ken – oh, blow Ken, she told herself irritably. He had caused quite enough trouble already. There was no sense in letting him cause any more. School was another thing, though. She could never meet Mary as a friend in those surroundings.

Fanny glanced into the bathroom as she crossed the landing but the man in a boiler suit was drinking tea from a thermos flask, and did not see her.

Mrs Mallalieu knocked at Mary's door and entered, bearing a tray and breathing heavily.

'I brought you – some lunch,' she announced between gasps.

'Oh, that *is* kind of you.' Mary sat up and smoothed out her sheets for the tray, on which was a plate of sardines on toast, two Marie biscuits and a cup of tea. Mrs Mallalieu sat down heavily on a chair.

'That girl who came. Was she – a health visitor?'

'Fanny? Oh, no. She's one of the girls I teach.'

'Oh.' Mrs Mallalieu looked unhappy. 'I thought she was a health visitor. Or from the Social Service.'

'No, nothing like that.' Mary began to eat the sardines on toast.

'You don't have – benefits? Or anything?'

'Benefits? Oh – money!' Mary laughed. 'No, it's all right, Mrs Mallalieu. Teachers get paid when they're ill.'

Mrs Mallalieu was relieved. 'I didn't want to trouble you, dear. But I *have* had tenants who' – wheeze – 'got behind with the rent. And that is very embarrassing. For every-one.'

'Yes, of course.' Mary took a sip of tea. 'Actually, I was going to tell you, Mrs Mallalieu, I may be moving before long.'

'A month's notice I'll need,' said Mrs Mallalieu promptly.

'And a month's notice you'll get,' returned Mary. 'I'm look-ing for a flat to share with a friend, you see, and you know how scarce they are. It might be ages before we find one. Or I might even change my mind.'

'If you were a nice young married couple, now,' said Mrs Mallalieu thoughtfully, 'my sister in Sheen has a place. But only one bedroom. For two girls it wouldn't be suitable.' There was an unspoken question in Mrs Mallalieu's beady stare and Mary hesitated for a moment. Then she said firmly, 'No. Sheen is too far away, I'm afraid. We're both teachers, you see, working here. Now, what do I owe you for the lunch?'

Mrs Mallalieu got ponderously to her feet. 'I think,' she said, 'we call it twenty pence for the sardines and the toast – real butter I used – and the biscuits. I won't charge you for the tea as I was making a pot for myself. I have my funny ways, I know but' – wheeze – 'nobody can say that Ida Mallalieu is mean.'

The telephone behind the cash desk rang and Colin answered it.

'Jackanapes Bookshop.'

'Is Mrs Anthony there, please?'

'If you'll hold the line one moment I'll put you through,' said

Colin, doing his parody of a personal secretary. 'Who is calling, please?'

'Miss Beacon's secretary, Critchlowe School. Miss Beacon would like a word with Mrs Anthony.'

'Thank you.' Colin put his hand over the mouthpiece and said gleefully, 'They're chasing you up about Fanny!'

'Oh, no!' Helen was dismayed. 'Is it the school?'

'The Headmistress herself. Tell her Fanny's got a sore throat.'

Helen put out her hand for the receiver. 'You're through,' Colin said into it sweetly, and handed it to Helen.

'Hello – this is Mrs Anthony.'

'Miss Beacon for you.' There was a click.

'Mrs Anthony? I just wanted a word about Fanny. She is away from school today.'

'Yes.'

'Is she unwell?'

'Sore throat!' hissed Colin. Helen flapped her hand at him. 'She seems very tired,' she said cautiously.

'I see. Are you aware that she left school without permission yesterday?'

Helen took a deep breath. 'Miss Beacon, I take it that you know about the personal troubles affecting Fanny's friend, Bobbie Rippon?'

'I do.'

'Well, I really do think that it's largely to Fanny's intervention yesterday that Bobbie is back at home. The whole thing has been quite an upset for everyone concerned, and when I say Fanny is very tired, I do mean just that.'

Colin raised an approving thumb.

'I appreciate your frankness, Mrs Anthony,' said Miss Beacon, 'and, to be equally frank with you, I do hope you will let me know if there are any further developments in this affair.'

'Yes, of course.'

'Good. You see, while appreciating that Fanny's motives are of the best, I feel that the welfare of the girls is essentially the concern of the school.'

'Oh, quite.'

'Fanny has a tendency to regard herself as being above the

law and this of course is a very undesirable attitude.'

'Yes.'

'I like to see the girls use their initiative, but when one individual starts to act completely independently of the rest of the community the results are seldom genuinely constructive.'

'Of course not.'

'Good. Well, we seem to understand each other, Mrs Anthony. You'll have a word with Fanny, will you?'

'Yes, I will.'

'And I'll see her at school on Monday?'

'Oh, yes, definitely.'

'Thank you so much. Goodbye.'

'Goodbye.' Helen replaced the receiver. Colin was grinning broadly.

'Did she tell you off?'

'Yes,' said Helen, 'I rather think she did. You know, I'd completely forgotten how bossy headmistresses can be. And do take that idiot grin off your face, Colin!'

'Sorry,' said Colin. But he found it very difficult to look suitably contrite.

'Here we are!' announced Fanny gaily, pushing open the back door. 'Bobbie's come to lunch!'

'Bobbie, dear, how are you?' Helen smiled but shot her daughter a meaningful glance across Bobbie's head which Fanny ignored.

'I'm all right,' said Bobbie. She felt, in fact, very exhausted and near to tears and wished that she had had the strength to resist Fanny's pressing invitation. 'I mustn't be long, though.'

'No, of course not. Lunch won't be a minute. There's shepherd's pie in the oven and I'm just heating some frozen peas to go with it.'

'How do you do it?' Bobbie was overwhelmed by Helen's energy and efficiency. 'You go out to work, don't you?'

'Oh, it's just a question of organising,' said Helen.

'Oh, she's efficient, is our Mumsie,' said Fanny.

'Don't you *dare* call me that!'

'Call you what?' inquired Stewart, coming into the kitchen. 'Oh, hello, Bobbie.'

'Hello.'

'Mumsie! Can you *think* of anything worse?'

'It sounds rather cosy. What about a sherry?'

'In the middle of the day?' queried Helen.

'Why not? It's my free afternoon and you're not likely to lay your customers flat on a thimbleful of amontillado. Fanny?'

'Yes, please.'

'Bobbie?'

'Oh, no.' Bobbie was thrown into confusion.

'Go on, Bob,' said Fanny, 'you'll love it. Just like Christmas. Sherry always makes me think of paper hats and holly.'

Stewart put a glass into Bobbie's hand. 'Just have a sip. No need to drink it if you don't like it, but I think it's just what you need.'

Very cautiously, Bobbie tasted it, then looked relieved. 'It's rather nice. Warm.'

'I want to go to Italy,' announced Helen.

'Don't we all,' said Fanny.

'No, I mean it. There's one of those literary meetings next month, in Venice.'

'Venice is ghastly,' said Stewart. 'Crumbling into its own stinking canals, and it smells worse than Merthyr Tydfil.'

'All the more reason to go, before it disappears completely.'

'When are you off, then?' Stewart sat down at the table, refusing to be ruffled.

'Thirteenth to the twentieth. And I really am going.'

'But that's in the middle of school term!' said Fanny. 'I'll never get up in the mornings!'

'That,' said Helen, 'is your problem.' She drained the peas in a cloud of steam. 'Bobbie, will you sit over there beside Fanny?'

Stewart watched the girl as she moved round the table to sit down. The sherry had brought a little colour to her face but there was an uncertainty in her movements which spoke of continued shock and she looked generally underweight and tired.

90

'You know Dr Robinson, don't you, Stewart?' said Fanny.

Stewart accepted a plate of shepherd's pie and looked at his daughter suspiciously. 'Yes, I do. Why?'

'What's he like?'

'Oh, not a bad old stick. A bit of a Calvinist, believes in the demon drink – worked for years in a tough part of Glasgow. That's enough to make anyone sign the pledge.'

'He's Bobbie's doctor.'

'Fanny!' Stewart was very annoyed. 'That's naughty of you!'

'I know, I know, professional opinions and all that. I'm sorry, but Bob happened to say her mother didn't like old Robinson much and I just wondered why.'

The scheming minx is up to something, thought Stewart. He frowned at his daughter but she returned his stare with an untroubled gaze and calmly began to eat her shepherd's pie.

'How *is* your mother, Bobbie?' asked Stewart.

'All right, thank you,' said Bobbie.

'Apart from lacerated hands, that is,' Fanny put in. Bobbie blushed violently and Stewart, trying not to smell a rat, said, 'Oh, dear. I suppose that's where Dr Robinson came in, did he?'

'No, he didn't. Poor old Bob was tearing up pillowcases in the middle of the night to make bandages and for all we know her mum's hands are still stuck full of broken glass.' Fanny glanced at Bobbie, whose face was hidden as she prodded without appetite at her shepherd's pie, and then gave Stewart a steady stare.

He cleared his throat uneasily but Helen said, 'How did it happen, then, this accident?'

'She dropped an empty squash bottle,' said Bobbie.

Fanny raised her eyebrows in elaborate irony and Helen, too intrigued to be discreet, said, 'Don't you think she ought to go down to Casualty, Stewart? Glass cuts can be very nasty, can't they?'

Stewart gave his wife a murderous look and they continued lunch in silence until Bobbie put her fork down and said, 'I'm awfully sorry but I don't feel very hungry.'

'That's quite all right, dear. I don't expect you do,' said Helen kindly. 'Would you like some fruit? Or there's yoghurt in the fridge?'

'No, thank you.'

'Then why don't you go into the sitting room while we clear up in here and I'll bring some coffee in for you and Fanny before I go back to the shop? It's nice and sunny in there and there's today's papers and the *New Statesman* and . . .'

'And *Petticoat*,' said Fanny, who was unapologetically devoted to magazines.

'All right.' Bobbie welcomed the chance to be alone. She was going to cry again at any minute and it was so dreadful, crying in front of other people. She got up awkwardly and said, 'Thank you,' and left the room.

Nothing was said until the sitting-room door was heard to close and then Stewart said, 'Fanny, *really* – what *do* you think you're doing?'

'It's much better for her to know that you know,' said Fanny obstinately. 'And anyway, I thought she might be glad to talk about it.'

'Well, you were wrong there,' said Helen. 'Poor little girl, I thought you were beastly to her. But what about this glass, anyway? What were you trying to say?'

'Bobbie's mother's an alcoholic. She fell down absolutely plastered with an armful of bottles and was crawling about in the mess on her hands and knees. I couldn't say so at the shop this morning because Colin was there and he'd have been round at the house like a shot, making things worse, but that's why I wanted Bobbie to come and stay with us for a bit.'

'Oh, I *see*,' said Helen. She thought for a moment and then added, 'But I still don't think it's your job to interfere.'

Fanny turned to her father. 'Stewart, couldn't you go and see Mrs Rippon? Not as a doctor – just as my father. Just sort of drop in.'

'M'm,' Stewart pondered. 'I suppose I might.' Helen, filling the coffee pot, smiled at the similarity between her husband and her daughter as they frowned at each other absently, cogitating.

'What a good thing the boys stay at school for lunch,' she said. Neither Fanny nor Stewart seemed to hear.

'I'll ring old Robinson,' said Stewart. 'But don't you ever use these bulldozing tactics again, Fanny, do you hear?'

'OK.'

'And don't say anything to Bobbie. You can't solve people's problems for them, you know. They have to do it for themselves.'

'But it's so awful for her.'

'Yes, I know, but she's young. She'll recover. Does she cry a lot?'

'Oh, never stops.'

'That's a good thing. It's a very natural process. The ones I don't like are the stiff upper lippers – the ones who try to get it all under control. They're the ones who have breakdowns. When's the funeral?'

'I don't know,' said Fanny, taken by surprise. 'I never thought about it.'

'Any relatives?'

'There's Bobbie's older sister and her husband.'

'Sensible, are they?'

'Oh – yes, very.'

'Good. As long as there's somebody.'

'Lord, look at the time,' said Helen, bustling about. 'I must get back. Fanny, will you take this coffee in for Bobbie?'

'Yes, of course. Do you want some, Stewart?'

'Later.' Stewart went out.

When Fanny took a tray of coffee into the sitting room she found Bobbie curled up on the settee.

'Coffee, Bob.' She put the tray down on a low table and turned to look at her friend. Bobbie lay still, her eyes closed and a damp, crumpled handkerchief loosely clutched in her hand. A shaft of autumn sunlight fell across her tousled hair and she breathed, a little noisily, through her open mouth. She was fast asleep.

Sylvia's bedside telephone rang. She stretched out an arm and picked it up clumsily. Her hands were very painful.

'Mrs Rippon?'

'Yes.'

'It's Stewart Anthony here.'

'Who?'

'Stewart Anthony. My daughter, Fanny, is very friendly with Bobbie. I just wanted to let you know that Bobbie is with us.'

'Bobbie with you. Why?'

'Fanny invited her to lunch.'

'I want her to come home,' said Sylvia. It was too bad of Bobbie, leaving her to wake up in an empty house. 'Tell her to come home.'

'She's fast asleep at the moment, I'm afraid,' said Stewart easily, 'but I'll bring her home the moment she wakes up. Are you alone?'

'Of course I'm alone.' Sylvia began to cry. 'My husband. . . .'

'I know,' said Stewart. 'Your husband died yesterday – I'm so very sorry. May I come round and see you?'

'Why?' Sylvia wiped her eyes on the back of her roughly bandaged hand.

'I'd like to see if I can do anything to help, even if it's just to get you a cup of tea or something.'

'All right. When are you coming?'

'Quite shortly.'

'Oh. Then I'd better. . . .'

'See you soon. Goodbye.'

Damn, thought Sylvia, fumbling the receiver back on to its rest, he sounds a nice man but what does he want? People keep ringing up. Marjorie rang up. Gordon rang up from work. School rang up. Awful, awful undertakers rang up. Funeral on Monday, I *can't*. Now this stupid man coming. Have to get up.

Shivering a little, Sylvia got out of bed and slowly put her clothes on.

The doorbell rang. It rang twice more before she went down and answered it. The man who stood on the doorstep was tall, with grey hair brushed forward and cut severely in a short fringe which made him look Roman. He was faintly untidy in a droopy tweed jacket and a polo-necked sweater and his grey eyes regarded her with a steadiness which she found simultaneously reassuring and alarming.

94

'I'm Stewart Anthony,' he said. 'Can I come in?'

'I've seen you before,' she said in an attempt at normal conversation as she stood back to admit him.

'Yes, I've brought Bobbie home once or twice but we've never really met. What a lovely house this is!'

Sylvia shrugged. The house was too big now. How could she and Bobbie fill the empty rooms? Silently she led the way into the sitting room. The curtains were still drawn and the dark room smelt like an unmade bed. Of course – it wasn't one of Mrs Webb's mornings.

'Sorry – I haven't been in here yet,' she said, fumbling with the curtains.

'Let me do that.' Stewart reached past her and pulled the curtains back, glancing at her bandaged hands but making no comment.

'Thanks,' said Sylvia helplessly. 'Would you like a drink?'

'I'd love one,' said Stewart.

Sylvia went to the cocktail cabinet and opened it with some difficulty. It was, she realised, going to be almost impossible for her to open a bottle. 'Perhaps you wouldn't mind helping yourself,' she said. 'I had a bit of an accident.'

'Yes, of course. What would you like?'

'Gin and tonic, please.' Sylvia perched irresolutely on the arm of a chair. The room looked frowsty with its flattened cushions and overflowing ashtrays.

Stewart was examining the bottles. 'I'm afraid you're out of luck,' he said. 'There are two empty gin bottles but there doesn't seem to be a full one. There's a little Cinzano – or there's whisky.'

'That'll do.'

'Whisky? With dry ginger?'

'Oh, I don't know. Anything.'

Stewart poured two drinks and gave one to Sylvia, who took it between both hands. 'What have you done to yourself?' he asked.

'Broke a mirror.' Sylvia laughed mirthlessly. 'Seven years' bad luck.'

'Have you had any treatment for it?'

'No, it'll be all right, it's just a few cuts.' Sylvia sipped her drink clumsily. It was sharply painful to move her fingers.

Stewart watched her. She winced as she put the glass down.

'Does that hurt?' he asked.

'Hurts like hell,' said Sylvia.

'You *are* having a bad time, aren't you?'

His sympathy was too much for Sylvia, who began to cry helplessly, her bandaged hands lying uselessly in her lap. She was still perched uncomfortably on the chair arm. Stewart got up.

'Come and sit down,' he said gently. 'Come on.' He led her across to the settee and supported her by the elbows as she sat down. He put her drink on a coffee table beside her and took a Kleenex from the half-used box on the floor. Awkwardly, using her hands like paws, she blew her nose.

'Can I have a look at your hands?' asked Stewart. 'I don't know if Bobbie told you, but I am a doctor. It's up to you, though.'

Sylvia hesitated, then nodded. 'Please.'

The inexpert bandages were tightly knotted at the wrists and the frayed edges of the torn cotton had become inextricably interwoven. 'I'll need some scissors,' said Stewart. 'Just stay put – I'll get some from the car.'

He came back with his medical bag and carefully cut away the bloodsoaked dressings.

'My word,' he said as the injured palms were exposed. 'You've had a good old go at those.' He gazed with interest at the crisscrossing of cuts and scratches. Most of them were superficial but a deep jab in the left forefinger was still oozing blood and the ball of the right thumb was deeply split. A lumpy, bluish discoloration under the skin indicated the presence of a glass splinter.

Sylvia glanced down at her hands and closed her eyes. 'Could you pass my drink?' she asked faintly. Stewart held the glass to her lips and she gulped at it.

'You all right?' he asked. 'Not sick or dizzy?'

'I'll be all right.' She shut her eyes again.

Stewart went out to the kitchen for some water to clean

Sylvia's hands and when he returned she looked a little better.

'Sorry,' she said. 'It was a bit of a shock, seeing what I'd done. Bobbie looked after me last night and I didn't watch what she was doing – I can't stand that sort of thing.'

Stewart, seeing that Sylvia's glass was empty, refilled it and then set about dressing her hands. 'You broke a window, you said?' he asked casually.

Sylvia hesitated fractionally then said glibly, 'Yes, I tripped on the bedroom rug and went through the window with both hands. Stupid thing to do.'

Stewart finished dressing her left hand then took her right one between his own. 'Don't look if you don't want to,' he said, 'but this bluish lump here makes me think you've still got some glass in it.'

'Can't you get it out?' said Sylvia, her head averted.

'No. I can't tell by looking at it which way the glass is lying or how big it is. I'd need an X-ray to tell me that – and you can't carry an X-ray unit in a little black bag.'

Sylvia did not smile. 'Not hospital,' she said. 'Not so soon after David – it was so awful in that ward.'

'I know,' said Stewart. 'I do understand. But if David knew you had a nasty cut in your hand that needed attention, he'd want you to have it, wouldn't he?'

'He'd have been furious,' said Sylvia flatly. And, as Stewart pondered over the implications of this statement, she turned to him impatiently. 'Well, are you going to do this hand for me? I can't very well get on a bus with it pouring blood, can I?'

'I'll take you down in the car,' said Stewart, 'if you'd like me to, that is.'

Sylvia's irritation evaporated. 'You're very kind to me,' she said. 'I don't know why you should be so kind.' She reached for her glass and found that she could hold it in her newly dressed left hand. 'That feels much better,' she said. 'Would you like another drink?'

'No, thank you.'

'Oh, go on. Keep me company.'

'I won't be very good company if I get had up for drunken driving.'

Sylvia shrugged. 'Spoilsport,' she said. The words were fractionally slurred.

'Have you had anything to eat?'

'No. I'm not hungry.'

Stewart finished putting a loose dressing on Sylvia's right hand and repacked his bag. Then he looked up.

'Shall we go?' he asked.

Bobbie, half-waking, rolled over. Her elbow encountered a soft obstacle on her left hand side, unusual in a bed. Then she realised that it was not a bed at all but a settee and her elbow had collided with the back of it. She opened her eyes and saw Fanny, sitting on a low pouffe near the fire, studying a book by the light of a pink-shaded standard lamp. The curtains were still undrawn and outside, the trees were barely visible against the darkening sky. Fanny looked up.

'Hello, Bob! Woken up at last?'

'How long have I been asleep?'

'Oh, hours. Would you like some tea?'

'I don't know. Yes, I think so. What's the time?'

'Five-ish.'

'Oh, Lord!' Bobbie sat up, panic-stricken. 'I must go home. Mum will be in an awful state!'

'It's all right. Stewart went to see her. He took her round to Casualty to get her hands seen to – he rang up from the hospital. They're probably home by now. I'll go and put the kettle on.'

The dull ache which Bobbie had felt since her father's death hurt more when she was alone. And there was something else, she felt sure. Something she ought to be doing.

'I've got the kettle on,' announced Fanny cheerfully, entering with a tray, 'and I've found some nice chocolate biscuits. We'll have a tea party.'

Colin. That was it. 'Fanny, it's Friday! Colin's coming round – I mustn't miss him!'

'Of course you won't miss him. Helen'll give you a lift home, or Stewart, whichever gets in first. You'll have hours to have a bath and do your face – no need to panic.'

And Fanny went out again, reappearing with the teapot. 'I'm

going out with Lee tonight, after rehearsal,' she said casually.

'Lee? That electrician chap?' Bobbie knew the Theatre Centre people only through Fanny's reports.

'Yes.'

'Is he nice?'

'Yes, I think he is, really, but I'd never thought about him before.' Fanny paused. 'Tell you something, Bob.'

'What?'

'You know Ken? Ken Olliphant?'

'Oh, yes, I saw him when I came to the last play.'

'Well, I've been absolutely nuts about him for ages. I never told anybody. I used to think about him all the time.'

Bobbie nodded. 'That's what I thought.'

'*Did* you?' Fanny was taken by surprise.

'Oh, yes. You were always saying things in his kind of voice and quoting his opinions. You seemed – just full of him.'

'I was.'

'Was?'

'He's fallen for Miss Ross.'

'*Our* Miss Ross? No! Oh, Fanny, what a shame!'

'No, it isn't,' said Fanny bravely. 'We had a long talk about it and it's better to know it's over.'

'Is that why you let Gordon . . .?'

'*No*,' said Fanny vehemently, 'that just sort of – happened. Bob, you can't think I engineered it?'

'Of course not,' said Bobbie quickly. 'It's just – well, Marjorie's my sister and Gordon's always been so nice and – it just seemed that there's nobody you can trust. Nobody at all.'

'I don't expect there is. Not completely. Does it matter?'

Bobbie looked troubled. 'Yes, I think it does, really. Things are so difficult all the time, I don't think I could manage without people to help.'

'Oh, they'll always *help*. Look at the school people – rushing about in a terrible tizzy, wondering if they've been too hard on you. Just wait until you come back – you'll be welcomed with open arms!'

'I can't come back till Tuesday. It's the funeral on Monday, you see. It's going to be awful. Fanny. . . .'

'What?'

'You wouldn't come, would you?'

'Of course I will.'

'What about school, though?' Bobbie suddenly lost courage. 'You've been away for two days – there'll be an awful row.'

'No, there won't. And if there is, it'll be a most enjoyable row, because moral right will be on my side. No, of course I'll come.'

Stewart came in. 'Hello! What a cosy scene! Is there any tea left?'

'I'll get you a cup,' said Fanny.

'Thank you.' Stewart sat down as Fanny left the room, and smiled at Bobbie. 'How are you feeling?'

'Much better, thank you. I've been asleep all afternoon – isn't that awful!'

'Not awful a bit. Do you the world of good.'

'Fanny said you went to see my mother.'

'Yes, I did. I popped her round to Casualty for an X-ray. How did she hurt herself did you say?'

'She dropped a bottle' said Bobbie, blushing.

Fanny came back and poured out a cup of tea for Stewart, who said, 'Thank you, love. Could you be a dear and cast an eye over the boys in the kitchen? They're doing something indescribable with a tin of pilchards.' He gave Fanny the ghost of a wink as he spoke and Fanny realised that she was being tactfully dismissed. Hiding her faint sense of resentment, she said, 'I expect they're trying to *flamber* them,' and went out, closing the door behind her.

Stewart stirred his tea and sipped it. 'I had a long talk with your mother this afternoon,' he said. Bobbie made no reply but watched him cautiously. 'She thinks she might go away for a little while,' Stewart continued. 'It's a very difficult time for her and she's not altogether well.'

'What's the matter with her?'

'Don't be alarmed. It's not really a physical illness at all. She's been under a strain for a long time and I think she needs some help in coping with it.'

Bobbie was silent. Looking at her tense face, Stewart realised that the girl looked frightened. 'What I was going to suggest,' he said, 'was that you might like to come and live with us for a while if your mother does decide to go. You'd be very welcome – and Fanny, of course, would be delighted.'

'Thank you,' said Bobbie. There was a long pause, then she asked, 'This place my mother is going to – what is it?'

'It's a kind of clinic,' said Stewart, 'down in Surrey.'

Bobbie gave a tremulous sigh and her eyes wandered away from Stewart, unfocusing in her old habit. Straitjackets, warders, madness, people screaming senselessly under the cedar trees as white-coated doctors approach across the shaven lawns. This was the end, then. Nobody was trustworthy. Nobody could even be guaranteed to stay alive. Mum. Oh, Mummy. Bobbie burst into tears.

'My dear, what is it?' Stewart put down his cup, levered himself out of his armchair and sat down beside Bobbie. He put his arm round her shoulders and she turned to him gratefully, burying her face against his jacket.

'There, chickie, don't cry – I didn't mean to upset you, I just thought a big girl like you had a right to know what's going on. It's entirely voluntary, you know, this place. If your mum does decide to go, it'll be of her own free choice and you can see her whenever you want to.'

'Can I?' She could not stop crying.

'Yes, of course. Did you think she was going to be shut away from you?'

Bobbie nodded.

'Look, my dear,' said Stewart, 'there's nothing much wrong with your mother. You've been worrying about her for a long time, haven't you? And now there are other people to worry for you. Real, expert worriers.'

'She's very nice really,' said Bobbie.

'Of course she's nice. She's a lovely person. But being a lovely person doesn't stop anyone from getting damaged. Your mother just needs some help, that's all.'

Bobbie nodded again, groping among the questions in her mind for one which she could ask this man.

'When—?' she began – but Helen flung open the door.

'Hello, Bobbie, you still here? My goodness, I thought you'd be at home getting ready for Colin. He's gone dashing off to put on his best bib and tucker. He even accepted a lift home so that he'd have more time. Shall I drop you back?'

Stewart glared at his wife but she continued unabashed, 'Saturday tomorrow. Come and spend the day with us and finish your tête-à-tête with Stewart. Fanny can cook the lunch. She's a jolly good cook, is old Fanny.'

Still with his arm round Bobbie, Stewart helped her to her feet. 'I'll run you home,' he said. 'OK?'

'OK.' Bobbie meant to sound relaxed and confident but her voice, through some obstinate weakness of its own, turned out to be no more than a croaky whisper.

Gordon opened the front door to Stewart and Bobbie.

'Come in,' he said. 'Where've you been, Bobbie? I was beginning to wonder if you'd gone off again.'

'I was at Fanny's,' said Bobbie. 'This is Dr Anthony, Fanny's father. He came round this afternoon to see Mum and tell her where I was. Didn't she tell you?'

Gordon shrugged. 'She's gone all depressed. She's sitting there staring into space and she won't speak to anyone. I think David's death is just about coming home to her. Would you like a drink, Dr Anthony?'

'No, thanks,' said Stewart. 'I must get back.'

'I met your daughter yesterday,' said Gordon conversationally. 'What a gorgeous girl, isn't she?'

Stewart smiled, but Bobbie shot Gordon a glance so charged with indignation that he felt sure Dr Anthony must notice it and wonder what it meant. Silly things, girls. Why did they always have to tell each other everything? Hastily he continued, 'Well, if you're sure you won't have a drink....'

'Quite sure,' said Stewart firmly. He had, he felt, spent quite enough of his off-duty time with the Rippon family – and besides, he had a few words to say to Helen.

'Bobbie's gone?' Fanny was surprised. 'But I thought she was in the middle of a heart-to-heart with Stewart. I was being all tactful.'

'There can be too much of this tact,' said Helen, head averted from the onions she was cutting up. 'I honestly do think that the more you sit about and brood, the more depressed you get. I know Bobbie's very upset – of course she is. But there's no sense in making her feel that her sufferings are special and different from anyone else's.'

'You're just being beastly,' said Fanny. 'And you needn't pretend to be so tough, because when Hannibal was run over you cried and said we'd never have another cat.'

'Yes, but I got over it,' persisted Helen, 'and we got Amadeus only ten days later. It's natural to mourn but one has to get it in perspective. Life goes on. Hand me that saucepan.'

'I'm not convinced,' said Fanny.

'Oh, to hell with you then,' said Helen amiably. 'Does anyone want potatoes with this or shall we make do with French bread? It's lamb chops and ratatouille.'

'I want chips,' said Matthew.

'Then get some out of the freezer and put them in an oven tray to thaw.'

Dominic raised his head from the shapeless construction he was working on and said, 'I *never* got over Hannibal.'

'You,' said Fanny, 'are such a righteous little beast that you'll probably fetch up as a bishop.'

'Actually,' said Dominic, 'I'm going to be an estate agent.'

'Mum,' said Bobbie, 'here's Colin. We thought we might go out for a bit.'

Sylvia turned her head slowly from the blank television screen. 'Colin.' She regarded him without much interest. 'Oh, yes.'

'I won't keep her out late, Mrs Rippon,' Colin promised. He was looking very handsome in a brown velvet jacket with a coffee-coloured shirt and a knitted silk tie, his red hair neatly brushed.

'No,' said Sylvia.

'Is there anything you'd like before we go?' asked Bobbie. 'Some coffee or something?'

'No.'

'Oh. Well, if you're sure it's all right. . . .'

Sylvia sighed sharply then switched on a radiant smile. 'I'll be fine!' she said with totally artificial brightness. 'So just you run along, the pair of you, and have a *lovely* time!'

Colin smiled back, 'Thanks! See you later, then.'

Bobbie, in a black sweater and a long cotton skirt, gazed at her mother with anxiety but Sylvia continued to smile. 'Off you go now!' she said. She did not meet Bobbie's eye.

Colin stopped outside the Taj Mahal restaurant. 'I don't know about you,' he said, 'but I'm ravenous. What about a meal?'

'If you like,' said Bobbie. 'I'm not awfully hungry.'

'Have you had any supper?'

'No.'

'Come on, then.'

The restaurant was almost empty and an attentive waiter ushered them into a corner table.

'I hope you like Indian food,' Colin said as the waiter handed them a menu each.

'Yes, I do. Dad took us sometimes.' The printed words blurred before her eyes and Bobbie clenched her teeth fiercely, trying to subdue the ache in her throat. She must not, must *not* cry here.

Colin watched her anxiously. 'Would you like a drink?' he asked.

'Please.' Bobbie was relieved to find the threat of tears receding. 'Could I have a sherry?'

'Yes, of course. I'll have one, too.'

While Colin ordered the drinks Bobbie stared at the menu, reading the unfamiliar names. Roghan josh, alu turcarri – she turned to Colin helplessly. 'I don't know what all these things are,' she confessed. 'You'll have to choose. Dad always did the ordering, you see.' It was all right this time. She could mention his name as long as she was prepared for it. Like all the other nameless threats in life, it was just a question of warding them off by taking precautions.

'That suits me,' said Colin. 'Half the pleasure in Indian food is combining it properly. You want something nice and spicy as a basis – a Madras meat curry or a vindalu perhaps, or a prawn one – do you like prawns? – then you have a contrasting taste in the vegetables. Let's see – we could have a brinjal bhaji and some tarka dal and – what about a bhuna qosht?'

'It sounds lovely,' said Bobbie. 'You seem to know an awful lot about Indian food.'

'I do,' said Colin matter-of-factly. 'I can't afford to eat out very often but I've got a marvellous Indian recipe book and I bought all the spices so I can cook curries at home. My mother thought it was a great laugh at first but now she's quite glad if I'll do an Indian meal for the family. They like it, too.'

'Do you cook all sorts of food, or just Indian?'

'Well, I'm specially interested in India. I feel I half belong there in a way. My great-grandfather was in the jute trade so he lived out there for years. My granny was born out there but she came back for school and married in Scotland and never went back. And now, of course, everything's changed.'

'Since self-government?'

'Yes.' Colin sounded regretful. The waiter brought their sherry and they sipped for a while, each eyeing the other covertly in the pink light which glowed from behind the cut-out shapes of temples punctuating the dark red flock-papered walls. Bobbie found a great pleasure in looking at Colin. She liked his wiry red hair and his serious eyes and the small cleft in his chin which made him look so pugnacious.

Pursuing his unspoken line of argument, she said, 'I don't think the British had any right to stay there, though. I mean, you can't just walk into a country and call it yours.'

'No, of course not. The place belongs to its own people – I'm the first to admit that. But there must have been a magic about it all the same, back in the early days. Just think of the excitement of discovering a new continent – but a continent that had thousands of years of its own history. The princes, you know, had the most fabulous palaces and jewels and art treasures. My great-grandfather used to go to the durbars given by the Maharajah of his province – granny told me about it when I was a kid. She had an ostrich feather fan with a very long handle so that a servant on the ground could reach up to fan her with it when she was in an elephant's howdah.'

'It can't be like that now.'

'No. But India itself won't have changed. The hugeness of the country is the same and the religions are the same and it must be mysterious in a way, just as it always was.'

'Do you want to go there?'

Colin looked down at his glass before replying. 'Yes, I do. As a matter of fact – I haven't told anyone this yet, but I'll tell you – I've given Mrs Anthony notice at the shop. I've not decided quite what to do yet, but I know I've got to travel. I feel as if I'll burst if I don't.'

'Then you'd better travel,' said Bobbie with bleak humour.

Colin looked at her. 'I'm doing this all wrong. I didn't mean to say a word about it. I just wanted to take you out and have a nice evening and here I am, talking about going away before I even know you properly.' He took a deep breath. 'I think about you all the time, you know,' he rushed on. 'Even when I'm doing something else a part of my mind is seeing you and talking to you but that's just a kind of fantasy. And now that it's happening for real I'm mucking it all up. I must be mad.'

'I think it's very nice of you to tell me,' said Bobbie, surprised by her own calmness. 'I'd much rather know what you really think.'

The pink lights gave a little colour to her white face under the mop of dark hair. Colin put his hand over Bobbie's and stroked the narrow knuckles gently. 'You're so lovely,' he said. 'Can't you come with me?'

'I'm still at school,' said Bobbie. 'I must stay next year at least, and get some O-levels.' Astonishingly, she found that she was considering the idea of going away with Colin quite seriously. With a new-found wariness, she told herself not to believe this dream. Dreaming was dangerous. Dreaming made you vulnerable. Dreaming was always punished. She smiled at Colin and said, 'You'll meet some Indian princess and fall under her spell.'

'I won't! Look, I'll admit it, you're not the first girl I've been interested in, not by a long chalk, but you must believe me, I've never met anyone like you. You – you *haunt* me, Bobbie!'

The waiter, unheard in his approach across the carpet, rattled some dishes on his trolley discreetly and Bobbie and Colin both laughed. The waiter smiled but his eyes remained impassive. The steaming array of aromatic dishes smelled delicious.

'Thank you,' said Colin, 'if you'll just leave everything we'll help ourselves.' The waiter bowed and withdrew as silently as he had come and Colin, serving spoon poised, turned to Bobbie. 'I've promised Mrs Anthony that I'll stay until after she gets back from a trip to Venice next month,' he said earnestly, 'and by then we'll be into the Christmas rush so it wouldn't be fair to leave her with all that. Then there's stock-taking in January, so it'll be some time before I can actually go. It's not as if I'm rushing off next week.'

'No,' agreed Bobbie. 'Look, don't let this lovely food get cold.'

They shared out the food, Bobbie taking only tiny amounts of each dish, and Colin ordered lager to drink with it, assuring Bobbie that wine was quite the wrong thing to go with curry.

Colin watched her with amusement as she picked up the big glass in both hands and drank from it. She put it down and said rather breathlessly, 'It's nice! Sort of bitter and fizzy – and a bit lemony.'

'That's right,' said Colin. He ate for a while in silence, then sighed contentedly and said, 'M'm, that's good. Are you enjoying it?'

'Yes, I am,' said Bobbie, sounding rather surprised. 'All the things taste so different from each other, don't they? And so fresh. It's the first proper meal I've had for ages, now I come to think of it.'

'Then I'm glad I brought you here. I think it's a super place.'

'Do you come here a lot?'

'Well, no. As a matter of fact it's the first time I've been inside it,' Colin admitted. 'I've looked at the menu quite often and thought it looked a nice place to take somebody special. It's been waiting for you.'

Bobbie smiled, pleased by the compliment.

'Your mother was very nice to us tonight, wasn't she?' Colin went on. 'She didn't seem to mind me taking you out a bit.'

'She may be going away soon,' said Bobbie. 'Dr Anthony's arranging for her to go to some sort of clinic – just for a while.'

Colin looked at her and Bobbie returned his gaze with un-flinching directness. 'I'm sure it'll be a good thing for her to do,' he said. 'Don't you? Really?'

'I hope so.'

'What are you going to do, though? You can't stay all by yourself in an empty house. Look, why don't you come and stay with us?'

'It's very sweet of you, but I'll probably stay with Fanny.'

'But Mrs Anthony's going to Italy,' objected Colin. 'There'll be nobody to look after you.'

This thought had already occurred to Bobbie but she told Colin, as she had told herself, 'I don't need looking after! It'll be fun helping Fanny to run the house.'

'Maybe,' said Colin, unconvinced. 'But I still don't think it's right.'

'Finish up that bit of prawn stuff,' instructed Bobbie, 'and the rice. Isn't it a lovely yellow colour!'

'Saffron,' said Colin. 'It's made from the stamens of a wild crocus, did you know? Buddhist monks use it to dye their robes.'

'*Do* they?' Bobbie sounded brightly interested. Colin's Indian dream-land was a far better topic of conversation than the problems of her own immediate future. 'I wish I was a monk,' she said, interrupting Colin's dissertation on crocus culture. 'They must lead such wonderfully simple lives.'

'I suppose they do. Narrow, though.'

'Or a crocus,' Bobbie continued dreamily. 'Just think of being a crocus, with nothing to do except open your petals in the sun and close them when the cold wind blows. Oh, I'd love to be a crocus.'

'That's understandable,' said Colin, 'specially after the last few days. But I'd hate it.'

'What'll you have?' asked Lee.

'Vodka and lime, please,' said Fanny. She was enjoying herself immensely.

'Right. See if you can find somewhere to sit – there's a chap just got up over there. I think he's going.' Lee indicated a distant table and pushed his way to the bar.

''Allo, darling!' The man Lee had seen leered at Fanny as she approached. His face was very red and he was perspiring profusely. 'Come to sit with me, have you?'

'We thought you might be going,' said Fanny.

'So I am, darling.' The man guffawed and rolled his eyes in the direction of the Gents. 'We all have to, don't we, from time to time? I'll be back, though, so don't go away, will you? Just sit down there and – here, you haven't got a drink. What are you drinking?'

'My friend is getting me one.'

'Your friend.' The man leaned closer to Fanny. 'Do I *know* your friend?'

'No, you don't,' said Fanny firmly. 'And if you stand there much longer, you'll probably burst.'

'Christ,' said the man, suddenly looking agonised, 'so I will.' He retreated hastily and Fanny grinned happily. What a splendidly *real* encounter! That was the sort of thing which no amount of education could give you.

Lee reappeared with the drinks and said accusingly, 'You're one of *those* girls.'

'One of what girls?'

'The sort you can't leave for two minutes before she's chatting up someone else. Cheers.'

'Cheers. But I'm not! I was being all cool and dignified. *He* was doing the chatting.'

Lee licked some Guinness froth off his upper lip and said, 'I'm not surprised. Do you know you're one of the sexiest girls I've ever seen?'

'Am I?' Fanny was vastly intrigued. 'Why?'

'It's your look of being clean and incorruptible. I think.' Lee studied her with his head on one side. 'And the way your mouth curves up from the corners to the middle so that you're always pouting a bit, like a cherub.'

'Ugh! That sounds repulsive!' said Fanny, laughing. Lee watched her mouth as she spoke.

'Gorgeous,' he murmured. 'You've got such marvellous teeth, too. Cor, you stir me up like a cup of tea, you do. D'you know that?'

Fanny laughed again, not at all sure what to say.

'I mean it,' Lee persisted. 'And I bet lots of men have looked at you and thought just the same. So what's the harm in saying what you think?'

'None at all,' said Fanny, feeling herself on more familiar ground. 'I think people ought to be free to say exactly what they think, all the time.'

'Specially about sex,' said Lee, egging her on.

'Not specially, but just as much. I mean, why do people make such a fuss about sex? You don't *have* to have babies or VD.'

'I wish you weren't still at school,' said Lee.

'So do I,' agreed Fanny whole-heartedly. 'But it doesn't *matter*, does it?'

'It does, in a way. I mean, how old *are* you?'

'How old d'you think?'

'I don't know – sixteen? Seventeen?'

'Something like that. So?'

Lee shook his head. 'It's like knowing two different people. When I see you in school uniform I feel like a baby-snatcher but the way you look tonight, I'd be trying to get you into bed by hook or by crook – if you weren't at school.'

'But that's ridiculous! It's such a rotten reason to give. It's treating me as if I wasn't a person at all!'

Lee put his beer down on a table, straightened his jacket, clicked his heels with great formality and said, 'Miss Anthony, will you sleep with me?'

'No.'

'Why?'

'Because I don't want to. Not yet, anyway. But it's nice to be asked. Thank you.'

Lee grinned. 'You're welcome! But just wait until you've left school, that's all!'

'Oh, *Lee*! You haven't taken the slightest notice!'

'There's my feelings to be considered as well as yours,' said Lee with pretended indignation, 'so belt up and have another drink.'

'Yes, please,' said Fanny.

As soon as Lee had gone, the man with a red face came across to Fanny, spilling beer a little from a full pint mug. 'I've been watching you, darling,' he said. 'You know, you're a very nice girl. Who's that chap you've got with you, darling? Skinny chap. Whoever he is, he doesn't deserve you. Why don't you let me buy you a drink?'

Fanny leaped forward confidentially. 'That chap I'm with,' she said, 'is the Southern Counties Karate champion. And what's more, he's my husband. And if he thinks you're messing me around, he'll kill you,' she snapped her fingers, 'just like that.'

'I've heard that tale before, darling,' said the red-faced man. 'That's what they all say.' But, as Lee approached, he nevertheless beat a hasty retreat.

'What are you giggling about?' asked Lee. As Fanny explained, the main lights in the room went out to signify the approach of 'time', leaving only the strip lights behind the bar and the orange glow of the revolving table lamps which advertised a brand of bottled beer.

'I *love* pubs,' said Fanny.

'Oh, they're a good thing,' Lee agreed. 'Except at closing time, that is. Come back to my place for some coffee?'

'No, thank you.'

'You know, for all your brave talk, you're as po-faced as a chapel hat peg,' said Lee. 'One whiff of seduction and you're off back to your mum.'

Fanny refused to be provoked. 'Come back to *my* place for coffee?' she suggested.

'And meet Mummy?'

'Don't be nasty. She's all right.'

'How far is it?' asked Lee. 'Walking distance from here, or should we go in the van?'

Fanny thought of the warm, oily-smelling intimacy of the van and paused, but only fractionally. 'Oh, we'd have to go in the van,' she said.

Lee finished the rest of his Guinness in a long, uninterrupted draught, and wiped his mouth with the back of his hand. He stared into the empty glass for a minute and then said, 'I'm all right really, you know.'

'Of course you are,' said Fanny, not sure what he meant.

'You mustn't mind what I say. What I mean is – well, I'd never really push it. Coming out with me – you'll be OK.'

'Oh, Lee! You *are* sweet!' Fanny was secretly relieved and found his stumbling declaration very touching. 'And you will come back for coffee, won't you?'

'I'd love to,' said Lee.

Colin and Bobbie took the long way home. It was a cold night with the smell of dead leaves and frost in the air but they walked slowly, arm in arm, warmed by the time they had spent in the restaurant and by the spicy food which lay comfortably inside them. They had talked inexhaustibly, each of them finding the other delightful both as a talker and listener. Nothing had seemed ridiculous or trivial; no experience, whether real or imagined, was insignificant.

'It's what happens to you inside your own head that counts,' said Bobbie. 'Even with things like somebody dying, it's not the death itself that makes you feel so awful – it's the way you can't stop hurting yourself.'

Her arm, looped through Colin's, tightened convulsively and she turned her face away. He stopped and drew her close against his shoulder.

'It's very early yet,' he told her. 'You can't hurry it. In time you'll get outside it. You'll weave it in with all the other things that have happened to you.'

Bobbie looked up. 'You know, don't you? How do you know?'

'I had an elder brother, Allan. He was killed on a motor bike when he was seventeen, five years ago. Did Sandie never tell you?'

'No. She's never mentioned it.'

'Perhaps not. She was only eight when it happened and she seemed to accept it all right, but you can't tell. It was the effect on my mother that was so dreadful. It was as if she'd died too, in her mind. She used to sit and stare at nothing, with her hands in her lap, and we'd all be hungry and she simply didn't notice.'

'Did she ever get over it?'

'Yes, in a way. My father had been doing the cooking for us and one Sunday she took the potato peeler out of his hand and said, "I'll do that." And then she worked so hard after that, cleaning and scrubbing and polishing, it was almost frightening. And she dug the garden over and planted so many lettuces we supplied the whole road with them. I don't think she feels the same but she's managed to go on living – for us, I suppose.'

'You need somebody,' said Bobbie.

They came to the footbridge and climbed up the wooden steps in silence.

'This is where we met,' said Colin. 'I nearly knocked you flat.'

'It was my fault. I wasn't looking where I was going.'

'Neither was I.'

'We met in our dreams,' said Bobbie.

Colin stopped and embraced her again, fascinated by her smallness and fragility. 'You're like a little bird,' he said. 'You've got light little bones, like a robin.'

'I've come home to roost,' said Bobbie contentedly – and instantly the impermanence of Colin's presence struck her like mocking laughter. For a moment she was tempted to beg him not to go and, as if reading her innermost thoughts, Colin said gently, 'I shan't go for ages, Bobbie. Maybe never. It's only a dream.'

'Don't say that!' Bobbie was aghast. 'If you give up your dream because of me then it's all spoilt. That's what happens to people, they start to belong to each other and the belonging spoils everything because they give too much up.'

'But we won't spoil it for each other because we *know* about it,' said Colin positively. 'We won't make a prison for each other. We'll be the first really free people.'

'Will we?'

'Of course we will! We can do *anything*! All we need is energy and courage and – and....'

'And dreams,' said Bobbie.

'And dreams.'

They walked on, down the steps and along the dark alleyway, and came out into the lamplit road.

'What's the time?' asked Bobbie.

'About eleven, I think.' Colin peered at his watch. 'Ten past.'

'Goodness. We said we wouldn't be late.'

'We're not late,' Colin protested. 'And anyway, your mother won't mind.'

'We mustn't be too long though.' Bobbie began to walk more purposefully.

'Don't worry about your mother too much,' advised Colin, responding to Bobbie's shift of mood with a more practical attitude. 'If she's made the decision to take herself in hand things'll be much better, won't they?'

'I suppose they will.' Bobbie was beginning to feel a troubled desire to get home.

'Here we are. It's been a lovely evening.' Colin kissed her but felt the tension in her body. He began to share her anxiety and glanced uneasily at the house.

'I'd better go in,' said Bobbie.

'All right. I'll see you again soon, won't I?'

'Yes, soon. Ring me?'

'Of course I will.'

There was constraint between them suddenly. Bobbie kissed Colin on the cheek like a child kissing its father goodnight, then turned and ran indoors.

'And did you have a Nice Time?' Sylvia's voice was heavy with irony. She elbowed the kitchen door shut behind her and leaned back against it.

Bobbie's heart sank but she said bravely, 'Yes, I did, thank you.'

'I didn't,' said Sylvia heavily. She glared at her daughter.

'It's very lonely here. It won't matter to you, of course, you've got your own life to lead, you can toss aside these little things like the death of your father, as long as you've got somebody to kiss you and cuddle you. I saw you!'

Marooned beside the breakfast bar, Bobbie felt frozen with hopeless depression. Sylvia moved across to the sink and dropped her cigarette into the little pool of water round the plughole. 'Why don't you say something?' she demanded. 'You stand there looking dopey – God, what a sight. To think that I should be lumbered with a white-faced brat like you!'

'I didn't ask to be born.'

'Of course you didn't ask! Even if you could have asked, you wouldn't. You've never asked for anything, have you, that's the trouble with you, you're such a sneaky little bitch, creeping about trying to please everyone. If you'd ever stood up and *asked* for what you want, I could say, "That's my daughter!" and feel proud of you.'

'Mum, please don't be so cross. I'm sorry I went out, but you didn't seem to mind too much.'

Sylvia shrugged impatiently. 'Oh, come in the sitting room for Christ's sake. I haven't got my cigarettes in here.'

Bobbie followed her mother across the hall. She had intended to go straight to bed but clearly it was impossible to make any such move at present. Sylvia lit a cigarette and replenished her glass from a half-full bottle of gin.

'That funny boy of yours,' she said more conversationally, 'what's his name?'

'Colin.'

'Colin. He fancies me, doesn't he? Did he mention me when you were out?'

'He said you seemed very nice tonight or something like that.'

'I thought he would.'

'But he wasn't thinking about you, not in that way. He just meant he was glad you didn't mind being left alone.'

'Never mind what he meant. He was thinking about me. He's too young as yet to know what he really wants. I knew by the way he looked at me how he felt.' Sylvia sighed happily and Bobbie could not contain her fury.

'You've got it all wrong! Colin isn't interested in you a *bit* – how could he be? You're just trying to spoil it all!'

'Then why should he mention me? A young man taking a girl out for the first time ought to be thinking of her, not of her mother.'

'He wouldn't have mentioned you at all only I happened to say you were going away for a bit and Colin asked me to go and stay at his house. He *was* thinking of me.' Bobbie was too anxious to protect the memory of her beautiful evening to notice her blunder.

Sylvia stared narrow-eyed at her daughter in dreadful silence. Then she said slowly, 'You – told – *him*? About *me*? You told him *that*?'

Totally unexpectedly, she took a quick step towards Bobbie and slapped her hard across the face. 'You little bitch!' she hissed. 'You really sink low, don't you?'

Bobbie, her eyes watering from shock and pain, saw with added horror that the force of the blow must have opened the wound on her mother's hand, for blood was soaking through the pink adhesive plaster on her palm. Sylvia, unnoticing, drained her glass and refilled it angrily, adding no tonic water. She rounded on Bobbie, who flinched.

'And just what made you imagine that you can shove me off into some lousy loony bin? Just what?'

'Dr Anthony said—'

'Hah! That interfering fool! Look, I'd tell him anything to shut him up. He's a bloody sanctimonious do-gooder and he can damn well mind his own business.' Sylvia was becoming incoherent. 'My life is *my* life. Not his. Not yours. Not your stupid Colin's. Mine.'

'I know, Mum. I never said. . . .'

'Oh, yes, you did. Sneaking round complaining to your nasty little boyfriend. Spreading tales about me. Nasty, nasty tales.' She began to cry. 'And I'm all alone. Nobody to take care of me. David's gone. And he didn't care. Wouldn't have gone if he cared. Didn't even want to stay alive.' She buried her face in her hands and wept.

Bobbie watched her for a little while with a curious detachment. The side of her head felt numb from the blow Sylvia had struck her, but her anger had gone. She regarded her mother with a kind of pitying indifference which was new to her. 'You'd better go to bed,' she said.

'Oh, Bobbie!' Sylvia looked up, tear-blotched and grotesquely blood-streaked, pitifully collapsed. 'Bobbie, darling, you're all I've got and I'm so beastly to you. You know I don't mean it, don't you? You know you're all I've got.' Her words tumbled over each other. 'You won't leave me, Bobbie, will you?'

'No,' said Bobbie stonily, 'I won't leave you.' It was a ritual which she had gone through on many previous occasions but this time she found an inner core of resistance. Silently she added, in slow, deliberate words, one day I will leave you. Not yet, but one day.

'I do love you, Bobbie, I really do.'

'I know.' She need not be the helpless recipient of her mother's abusive love for ever. There would be some end to it, at present unknowable but certain all the same. 'Go to bed,' she repeated with more confidence. 'And leave your glass down here. You don't need that.'

'No,' agreed Sylvia, 'don't need that. Silly glass.' Petulantly, she threw the glass at the fireplace in a feeble caricature of bravado. It fell unbroken on the hearth rug and rolled away under the television set, spilling gin as it went.

'Come on,' said Bobbie. 'Upstairs.' She tried to assist her mother to get up but Sylvia swept aside the proffered arm.

'Don't need your bloody help,' she said, struggling to her feet. She left the room in an unsteady rush and Bobbie heard her stumble twice on the way up the stairs. The bedroom door banged and then there was silence.

'Goodnight!' called Bobbie. As she had expected, there was no reply. The television set, which had been on unnoticed, was playing the National Anthem. For a moment Bobbie felt overwhelmed by solitude and almost obeyed an impulse to go and ring up Fanny. But no. Fanny, she remembered, had gone out with Lee tonight – and in any case, it was too late to ring people up.

Bobbie switched off the television set and stared exhaustedly at the bright spot which appeared in the centre of its blank screen. Suddenly it seemed that she saw it as her father would have done. How often he must have stood here alone as she stood now, depressed and angry in the aftermath of a scene such as this! Ironically, it was only now, when it was already too late, that she felt able to know him as a real person. During his life he had seemed an outside presence. And now he had gone away to an unknowable, unreachable state of nothingness. Perhaps there were times when he had wanted to die. Bobbie did not know, but for the first time she could imagine that he might have done.

She moved slowly round the room, turning out the table lamp and the standard lamp and picking up the warm, sticky glass from the carpet. Death was not to be feared. Death was the only real perfection; the only certainty. Jesus had died. Maybe death was God.

At the door, Bobbie turned out the last light. The bright spot in the television screen glowed on, senselessly.

6 Saturday

Fanny and Bobbie sat in the Tea Room which was up six-red-carpeted stairs behind the Sally Lunn cake shop, dipping Marie biscuits into their coffee. The glass-topped tables were made of wicker, gilt-painted, and the matching wicker chairs creaked to the sitter's every movement. A huge, dusty palm plant stood on a carved wooden stand in the corner and over the fireplace was a large panel of glazed tiles depicting camels and native porters in a style poised somewhere between a Sunday School picture and a Turkish Bath. Fanny perversely adored the place, which was a relic of the time when the High Street belonged to a country town rather than to a London suburb, and relished the fact that her fellow coffee-drinkers were always elderly ladies in felt hats, sometimes accompanied by grown-up daughters and by grandchildren who were reproved for gobbling the ices (served with a wafer biscuit in brown-patched electro-plated dishes on stalks) too fast for good manners. Men were very seldom seen in the Tea Room and most people of Fanny's age would not have dreamed of entering it, lacking as it did both chips and a juke box.

'Yes, it was a hoot,' Fanny was saying. 'He wanted me to go to his place but I wasn't having that so, just for a laugh, I asked him home to meet my parents. I thought he'd be off like a shot but he actually came! It was terribly funny, though. Stewart kept talking about electricity all the time and saying how he once gave himself a shock with an electro-cardiograph machine, and Helen was going on about the unions and saying she thought the big question before the nation was about workers' control of industry. You could see they were both leaning over backwards to be democratic.'

'What did Lee say?'

'Nothing, really. He kept looking from one to the other and raising his eyebrows and saying things like, "Go on?" and "Oh, really?" and the quieter he was the more they talked.'

'It sounds awful.'

'No, it wasn't, it was gorgeous! I think it's so lovely when you put people together who simply don't understand each other.'

Bobbie shook her head. 'I sometimes think you're a sort of sadist, Fanny. You like watching people getting into a mess and making fools of themselves.'

'Oh, Bob, I don't! I mean, I really like Lee. He's tremendously kind and he's got a super sense of humour and well, there's lots about him that really turns me on. I just enjoy watching people, that's all. I think they're so interesting.'

'And funny.'

'All right, yes. And funny. I think most things are funny, in a way.'

'You don't think school's funny. You're always getting cross about it.'

'Oh, *school*. The trouble with them is, they won't let anything *be* funny. The minute you don't take one of their piddling little rules perfectly seriously they get absolutely hysterical. Talk about not seeing the wood for the trees! All this fuss about details is enough to narrow the mind for life, drawing margins and wearing ties and—'

'All right,' said Bobbie tiredly. 'I didn't mean to set you off.'

Fanny looked at her friend with concern. 'Sorry, love,' she said. 'Are you feeling a bit yucky today?'

Bobbie nodded. 'A bit.'

'Poor old thing. Hey, how did you get on with Colin? I was so busy chatting about my own affairs I quite forgot about you. Did you go out?'

'Yes, we had an Indian meal. It was super.'

'What about your mum? Did she mind you going out?'

'Yes, she minded.'

'Oh, Lord. Was she beastly? Never mind, she'll be going off to her clinic soon, won't she? We'll have lots of fun, Bob. If you come to stay when Helen's away it'll be great. We can cook some really hilarious meals.'

Bobbie stirred her half-empty coffee cup round and round slowly, staring down at it. 'She's not going,' she said.

'Not going? But why, Bob? Stewart said he thought she was all set to make a real fresh start. He said when something ghastly happens like this about your father it sometimes starts people off on a whole new phase of their lives.'

Bobbie put the spoon carefully into the saucer and propped her chin on both hands. She couldn't cry here, damn, oh damn.

'There's a gorgeous old bird over there with her hair in a snood!' said Fanny tactfully. 'I think she must be a fortune teller on her day off. She's having a toasted tea-cake all smothered in butter and she's cutting it into *tiny* bits, ever so delicate, and wiping her fingers on a lace hanky. She'll have to throw it away, I think, otherwise she'll have a buttery hand-bag.'

'Oh, Fanny!' Bobbie laughed weakly through her tears. 'You are an idiot!'

'Have some more coffee,' said Fanny. She peered into the straight-sided silver-plated coffee pot. 'Yes, there's enough for one.' She poured it out. 'The milk's a bit chilly. Shall we be devils and order some more.'

'I'd better not. Mum was a bit upset last night and I think she'll want a bit of looking after today.'

'But what's going to happen, Bob? You can't go on like this.'

'I know. I won't have to, not for always.'

Fanny glanced at her friend in astonishment. This, for Bobbie, was revolutionary. 'You're going to marry Colin?'

Bobbie blushed. 'No, of course not.'

'He's nice, though, isn't he?'

'Oh, *yes*.'

'Well, then, what are you up to? You've got some fiendish scheme in your mind, I can tell.'

'Not really. It's just – well, there was a bit of a scene with Mum last night and I lay awake for hours, thinking about things. I just couldn't see what there was to live for.'

'There's Colin.'

'Colin wants to go to India. It's a sort of dream, but I think he'll go all right. He wants to make it come true, you see. And that's what started me thinking. I've got to do something *real*, Fanny. Dreams let you down.'

'What do you mean?'

'Well – you won't laugh, will you? – I used to have this dream about the green hill far away, and Jesus standing at the top in the sunset, and I'd think of it if things were horrid. The green hill was always there.' She paused.

'But—?' Fanny nudged gently.

'It was the Brethren, really. They made the Jesus dream perfectly real, you see. It wasn't a dream any more. It wasn't an escape. It was a day-to-day way of life. And I knew I didn't believe it. Not enough, anyway. I wasn't sure if I believed anything.'

'I don't see how anyone *can* be sure,' said Fanny.

Bobbie frowned. 'I think I believe in – nothing,' she said. 'I don't mean "not anything" – I mean that there's a sort of nothing at the beginning and the end of life, and, compared with that nothing, all sorts of things seem – well – *good*. Like just sitting here.'

Fanny nodded agreement.

'So I thought I'd be a nurse,' Bobbie rushed on, 'because although they see some nasty things, they're *real* things you can do something about.'

Fanny laughed. 'I'd hate it!' she said. 'Too many people telling you what to do.'

'But I'd belong somewhere,' said Bobbie. 'And I'd matter to someone, wouldn't I?'

Fanny looked thoughtful. 'You certainly would. You know, I think you may be right, Bob. You're so conscientious, you might be a marvellous nurse.'

A waitress in a frilly apron placed a folded bill on a plate at Fanny's elbow, brushing against her so slightly that it seemed accidental. 'Pardon,' she said.

Fanny looked up and saw that a small queue of people had formed by the door, waiting for tables. 'Oh, Lord,' she said, 'we'd better go. What a nuisance.' She picked up the bill and raked in her purse, and the waitress smiled apologetically.

'Sorry to chivvy you, dear,' she said, 'but people can get quite nasty sometimes, when they've been waiting.'

'That's quite all right,' said Fanny, counting out money on to the plate. 'I dare say I'd get nasty too. There.'

'Thank you very much, miss.'

Fanny and Bobbie walked through the crowded shop and out on to the pavement. It was a sunny morning and the street was full of Saturday shoppers.

'Have you got to go home, Bob?' asked Fanny. 'Come and have some lunch. Helen's half expecting you, so it's fine with her.'

Bobbie shook her head. 'Better not.'

Conversation was difficult in the jostling crowd and so Fanny turned into the first side street they came to, where small houses stood close behind their privet hedges. 'That's better,' she said as Bobbie joined her. 'I do hate being pushed about in crowds. If you trained to be a nurse, Bob, you'd live in, wouldn't you? So you'd have to leave home.'

'Yes, I suppose so.'

'And once you're trained, you could work wherever you liked. Abroad, or anywhere.'

'Yes.'

'You know, it's a very good idea. How old d'you have to be?'

'Eighteen, I think.'

'M'm. That leaves three years to fill in.'

'I'll stay at school and do A-levels.'

'You *have* got it sorted out, haven't you? Whatever started you on this nursing idea?'

'It was Sister Davis, when we went to see Dad. I was feeling so awful and she was so – solid, somehow. And so busy. All the nurses were. They didn't have time to think too much.'

'Have you told your mother?'

'Oh no.' Bobbie sounded alarmed.

'Well, I think you ought to. Tell her right now, and then she'll know where she stands.'

'Fanny, I couldn't! Not when she's so upset.'

'All the more reason. She'll start to depend on you otherwise, her one little companion, and it'll be much worse later. I won't have you being a martyr – martyrs are smug and boring and plain bloody stupid.'

Bobbie laughed her shocked laugh.

'And what's more,' Fanny continued, 'I shall hold a pistol to your head. If you haven't told her within – let's see – three days, I shall tell her myself. So there!'

'You wouldn't!'

'Oh, yes, I would. I'd ring up all innocent some time when I knew you weren't there, asking to speak to you, then say, 'Isn't it nice, Bobbie going to be a nurse? I *do* think it's sensible!'' And then the fat *would* be in the fire.'

'All right,' said Bobbie. 'I think you're beastly, but I expect you're right. I'll tell her tomorrow.' Butterflies of fear were chasing each other in her stomach.

'Why not today?'

'I might be seeing Colin. Oh!' Bobbie clapped a hand to her mouth.

'What?'

'He said he'd ring up. I do hope he hasn't rung and got Mum instead of me.'

'Not to panic. If he has, she's probably been charming. And if she wasn't, it won't worry him. He's quite tough, I should think.'

'Oh, yes,' said Bobbie a little sadly.

There was a pause and then Fanny asked, 'Are you really keen on him, Bob? Like I was about Ken?'

'I think I am,' said Bobbie, turning very pink, 'but it's silly, really. He's got all sorts of things he wants to do.'

'So have you,' said Fanny.

They reached the end of the narrow street and turned into Wilmot Road beside the timber yard, not far from the brick building where the Brethren lived.

'This place has seen some dramas in the last couple of days,' said Fanny with satisfaction. 'Police cars and lost girls and poor old Gordon with his eyes crossed with anxiety.' To her relief, Bobbie laughed. She didn't seem worried about Fanny's brief entanglement with Gordon any more.

They were level with the red brick warehouse and, as suddenly as a stone dropped into a still pool, a clear trumpet note broke out, was held, and then slid into a jazz phrase. The grubby, featureless street instantly assumed the poignancy of the blues, forlorn and yet resilient, and the rhythm implicit in the trumpeter's long, idle phrases caused both girls to sketch the ghost of a dance as they paused and gazed up at the anonymous frosted glass windows.

'It's Jeremiah,' said Bobbie a little huskily. 'I thought he'd be the one I'd like because he plays so beautifully, but he wasn't. Isn't it lovely, though?'

'It's terrific,' said Fanny. 'It makes everything *mean* something, somehow – if only one knew what.'

'They're so lucky,' said Bobbie, gazing wistfully at the building. 'Having such faith. It makes things much easier.'

'But isn't this enough?' Fanny spread her arms wide, encompassing the music and the street and the sky. 'This is here and now, never mind your old God. This is marvellous. What more could you want?'

'I don't know. Perhaps this is all there is.'

Fanny laughed. 'If there was anything more I think I'd die of over-stimulation, like a mouse in oxygen. No, I'll take the package deal, just the way it is.'

Bobbie made no reply. She listened, absorbed, to the music for a few minutes more, then shook her head as if to free herself from a spell. 'I *must* go,' she said, and started off at a rapid walk. Fanny ran a couple of steps to catch up with her.

'I'll come as far as the alley with you, then I'd better go home too. The boys want lunch early because Stewart's taking them to some awful engineering trade show at Earls Court. Will I see you tomorrow?'

'I don't think so. If I'm going to tell Mum about being a nurse it'll take most of the day to work up my courage.'

'Monday, then. The funeral.'

'Fanny – I've been thinking about that. I know this sounds awful but – I think I was silly to ask you to come. It'll cause an awful upset with Mum if I bring someone from outside the family.'

'Are you sure?' Fanny was secretly disappointed.

'Yes, I think so. It's going to be awful, but Marjorie and Gordon will be there.'

'You couldn't ask Colin?'

Bobbie shook her head. 'No, that would be disastrous.'

'Well, you know best. Pretend you're somewhere else if it all seems too dreadful. Think of us sitting on the floor at Assembly with the Beacon bird praying at the ceiling the way she does.' Fanny assumed a solemn face. 'Oh, Lord our Governor—' The incantation was too familiar to resist and Bobbie joined in, 'through whose good providence this school has been planted, make it as a field which the Lord has blessed. Bless our founders and our benefactors,' they chanted together, walking in step side by side, 'bless all those who work for us and all who love us—' They arrived at the alleyway which led to the footbridge and stopped.

'All who love us,' repeated Bobbie uncertainly. 'What comes next?'

'I've forgotten,' said Fanny cheerfully, 'but that'll do to go on with. Just keep saying it over and over again. It'lll keep your mind occupied.'

'Perhaps it will.'

They looked at each other for a moment.

'I hope you'll be all right,' said Fanny with sudden concern. 'I'll think about you.'

'Will you? I'll think about you thinking.'

'Are you coming back to school on Tuesday?'

'Yes, I want to come back.'

'Good. Well – see you Tuesday, then.'

'See you Tuesday.'

Bobbie turned away and began to walk down the alleyway towards the bridge. Very faintly, she could still hear the sound of Jeremiah's trumpet but as she climbed the steps the music had gone and she could hear nothing but her own footsteps. The prayer, too, had obstinately fled from her mind, leaving nothing but its last phrase which reiterated itself again and again in an unbidden echo of the voices which had left it unfinished. 'All who love us . . . all who love us. . . .'

It was, Bobbie thought, an insignificant, almost meaningless scrap of English with which to try and arm one's mind against disaster. But it would probably do.

TOPLINER REDSTARS for your enjoyment

by Stanley Watts

The Breaking of Arnold

A story about Arnold, who is leaving school with no idea what to do with his life. He meets Ruth, who is sophisticated and intelligent, and falls in love with her. He now has the incentive to apply to University.

by Patricia Windsor

The Summer Before

A story about a teenage girl's adjustment to the death of her childhood friend and lover.

by Louise Lawrence

Andra

The story of Sub-City One 2000 years hence and Andra, who is recovering from a brain-graft operation in which she received part of the brain of a boy who died in 1987. Andra begins to see her world from the donor's point of view, resulting in violent rebellion against the administrators of the City.

by Vadim Frolov

What It's All About

This novel is set against the background of present-day Leningrad. Its subject is Sasha, whose mother has disappeared with an actor from her touring company. Sasha is not told this, and the story shows his struggle to find the truth.

TOPLINER REDSTARS
GENERAL EDITOR: AIDAN CHAMBERS

The Doubting Kind

Part Two: All Who Love Us ...

This is the second part of *The Doubting Kind*. Lots of things
have already happened to Bobbie and Fanny in the first part
of the story, which is called *A Friend In Need*. Bobbie's
father has had a car accident following a quarrel with his
wife, Sylvia, and is still in hospital. Bobbie herself, half through
real causes and half through imagined ones, has run away
from school and taken refuge with the Brethren, a religious
group who live in an old warehouse.

Fanny, too, has had ups and downs, including a fear that
her loved and admired Ken Olliphant, who runs the Drama
Centre, is falling for Mary Ross, a young teacher at Bobbie and
Fanny's school. Compared with her concern about Bobbie,
however, Fanny's personal affairs seem insignificant. Her main
anxiety is to find out what has happened to her friend.

Also by Alison Prince

The Doubting Kind:
   Part One   A Friend in Need